The
DEVIL'S
KISS

The
DEVIL'S
KISS

USA TODAY BESTSELLING AUTHOR
GEMMA JAMES

Note To Readers

The Devil's Kiss is a dark romance with a BDSM edge that does NOT conform to safe, sane, and consensual practices. Includes explicit content and subject matter that may offend some readers. Intended for mature audiences. Book one in the *Devil's Kiss* series.

1. THE DECISION

"You wanted to see me?"

"Yes, shut the door, Kayla."

His tone issued a warning that echoed in my ears, and I almost jumped as the door clicked shut. As usual, his presence caused an unsettling tickle in my stomach. Gage Channing left no room for mistakes or excuses—every single one of his employees displayed their best behavior, or else. I shuddered to think of the woman he'd fired last week; she'd scurried from the building as mascara tracked down her cheeks.

"Sit down." He gestured to the leather chair in front of his desk.

I sat, crossed my legs, and forced myself to meet his gaze. He had a way of piercing people with his eyes. They were startling—the kind of blue that dolphins played in. I got the feeling he saw right through me, as if he'd known what I'd been doing and had bided his time until the perfect moment presented itself to pounce. Was that moment now?

He slapped a folder on the desk. "Do you know what's in here?"

"N-no, Mr. Channing."

"I'm disappointed, Ms. Sutton."

My heartbeat tumbled twice, then sped up. He rarely addressed me so formally, a fact which caused a fair amount of gossip in the office. Some speculated the boss had a thing for me, and others went so far as to claim we were screwing like rabbits after hours. "I'm sorry, I'm not sure what you're getting at." *Liar!* He'd found me out; I was sure of it.

"I'm referring to the ten grand you stole from Channing Enterprises." He opened the folder and pushed the evidence in front of me. Account statements. Ledgers.

Oh God...

"I trusted you, Kayla. I even promoted you to personal assistant, and this is how you repay me?"

"I was desperate." I swallowed hard as the reality of my situation threatened to choke me. He'd have me thrown in jail, and Eve...Eve would die without me by her side. "My daughter is sick. I needed money...please, I'll pay you back. Every penny." I lifted my head and faced his granite expression. "Just don't turn me in."

If he was affected by my plea, he didn't show it. "I don't plan to alert the authorities." He snapped the incriminating file shut. "But you're correct when you say you'll pay me back." He steepled his fingers and rested his chin on them. "There is something I want. I've had a contract drawn up outlining my terms, and if you want my silence—and the evidence destroyed—you'll sign it."

"What do you want from me?" My voice quivered, and when he flashed a devilish grin, I gripped the chair to keep from bolting.

Gage got up and rounded the desk. His body overshadowed mine as he knelt beside me. A line of stubble darkened his jaw, giving him an undeniable hint of danger. "I want you as my slave."

"Your slave?" My jaw dropped. Did I even want to know what that meant?

"Hmm, yes. My slave." He lowered his gaze to my mouth, then lingered on my breasts, and his inspection burned a hole through my blouse. In response, my nipples tightened underneath the silk. "Surely you've heard of BDSM," he added.

I screwed my mouth shut. I didn't like where this conversation was going at all.

"Bondage, discipline," he said, inching closer, "punishment." The last word he savored, as if fine wine dampened his lips. "I'd say you've earned quite a bit. Wouldn't you agree?"

"I can pay you back," I said. "It'll take time, but I'll get the money."

"I don't want your money." Warm and minty breath breezed across my lips, inviting my mouth to mate with his. I edged away and clung to the side of the chair.

"I want your submission," he continued, "absolute ownership of you and your body. That's what I want."

I worked my jaw, searching for the words to express my disbelief, but only ended up staring at him in stunned silence. The man could have any woman he wanted, and all it would take was a crook of his executive finger. "Why are you doing this?"

His face darkened. "I have my reasons."

"You're crazy if you think I'll agree to this."

"You're too gorgeous to waste away in prison." He placed a hand on my leg, right above my knee. I tensed, afraid to move, afraid he'd push his possession further if I resisted. "You know"—he gently slid his palm upwards —"the penalty for embezzlement in Oregon is up to five years."

My breath hitched as he grazed the skin underneath the hem of my skirt. "Don't."

He raised an eyebrow. "No?" Gage reached for the phone. "Are you sure?"

The futility of my situation spilled from my eyes. Upset with myself for displaying weakness, I wiped the tears from my cheeks. "Don't call."

As if I'd given him permission, he uncrossed my legs and wedged them apart. "I love natural redheads." He slipped his fingers under the edge of my panties and smoothed them over my crotch. "Are you just as red here?" he asked, grabbing a pinch of hair.

With a nod, I closed my eyes. My entire body tingled, and not in a good way. I couldn't believe my boss was doing this to me...in his office in the middle of a workday.

"I'm tempted to leave you natural, at least for a while. I want to see you first."

My face burned with humiliation, and it took

everything I had to keep my legs apart. I balled my hands until my fingernails bit into skin. "This is sexual harassment, you bastard. It's illegal, and so is blackmail."

He withdrew his hand, and by the time I looked up, Gage had reclaimed his seat. "Don't think of it as blackmail. Think of it as an alternative to prison. I'd much rather punish you myself." He opened another folder and slid the contents across the desk. "You either submit to me or go to jail. Either way, the decision is yours."

With unsteady fingers, I fiddled with the paperwork but couldn't bring myself to read his demands. "What exactly do you have in mind?"

"Let's start with the basics." He gestured toward the contract. "You'll be my submissive for the next six weeks, beginning immediately upon your signature. I prefer a live-in arrangement on the weekends. During the week I expect you to follow my rules." He leaned back in his chair and kept a steady gaze on me. "You'll come to work as usual, but under no circumstances will you flirt or date other men, or entertain or go out with friends—"

"What about Eve? I spend most of my time at the hospital."

"I'm aware of that, and I don't have an issue with you seeing her, but the weekends belong to me, understand?"

If I could shoot daggers with a single glance, he'd feel my pain. "What else?" I tossed the contract down and crossed my arms.

"I expect absolute obedience." The corner of his mouth curled. "I won't hesitate to punish you when necessary. Of course, you'll choose a safe word." He frowned, as if the idea didn't please him. "However, should you decide to use it, our contract will become null and void, and I'll turn you over to the police. If you speak with anyone about this, the same stipulation applies."

Tears of desolation dripped down my cheeks, and I no longer cared about hiding them. His ultimatum terrified me. I wasn't a stranger to abuse, but being someone's slave—in every sense of the word—was a terrifying concept. "Eve will wonder where I am on the weekends."

"She'll benefit from our agreement. I'm allowing you to keep the money, which in turn ensures she gets the treatment she needs. I understand it's experimental and that you don't have the luxury of time."

I narrowed my eyes. "How did you know about that?" I hadn't talked to anyone about Eve's treatment. It was too painful a subject, and the last thing I wanted were platitudes thrown in my face. The insurance had refused to cover it, and Eve was out of options.

"I have my sources." He leaned forward with a smirk. "I have vested interest in you, Kayla—ten thousand dollars worth. You're desperate, and I know you'll give me what I want because even though I'm giving you a choice, your love for your daughter won't."

"There's a hole in your logic. Even with the ten grand, I'm still short."

"You underestimate me. I'll pay for her medical bills in full. She'll be taken care of."

The bastard had me, and he knew it. "What will you

do to me?"

"It's all there in the contract…but to put it succinctly"—he leaned forward with a glimmer of excitement in the depths of his eyes —"whatever I damn please."

I forced my attention onto the papers. Certain words and phrases popped out: Flogging. Bondage. Nipple torture. Anal play. I stared at him, slack-jawed. "You'd hurt me like this?"

"Yes," he lowered his voice, and something about his deep timbre shot through me, "but there's a flimsy line between pain and pleasure."

"I think I'm gonna be sick."

"Decide now. I'm growing impatient."

"Please, Gage. Don't make me do this. Please, I'll—"

"You'll save your begging for later, preferably while on your knees." He held out a pen. "But either way, decide."

I glared at him. "Do I have a choice?"

"Of course, just as you have the option of backing out of our agreement whenever you wish." He tapped the pen against the desktop. "That's the beauty of this. The choice is yours."

"But if I don't agree, you'll turn me in and Eve won't get her treatment."

"Correct."

"That doesn't sound like much of a choice. That sounds like coercion."

"I want you, and I'm willing to cross a line to get what I want. Just as you did to save your daughter's life."

I snatched the pen from his hand and stabbed the paper with my signature, essentially signing over my soul to the devil incarnate. I'd only experienced this kind of claustrophobic captivity one other time in my life, and it was a time capsule of hell I'd buried deep in my memory. Would Gage unearth it?

"Excellent." He grabbed the contract and enclosed it in a safe. "And since today is Friday"—he scribbled something on a piece of paper—"here's my address. Go to BodyScape Spa first and ask for Glenda. I'll call ahead and make arrangements."

I moved toward the door, my steps heavy, as if he'd already shackled my ankles.

"Oh, and Kayla?"

I stiffened at the sound of his voice. "Yes?"

"I want you on my doorstep wearing nothing but a trench coat in two hours."

He was insane if he thought I was going to do that.

2. DETOUR

I gagged for what seemed like the tenth time and heaved more of my lunch into the toilet. I'd probably never eat chow mein again. Getting to my feet, I braced against the stall and closed my eyes. Gage was all I thought about. Nothing else penetrated past the haze in my mind. I tried to imagine him touching me…doing more than touching me, but my stomach rolled again at the thought.

I stumbled out of the stall, still shaking, but at least I'd stopped vomiting. Katherine, the receptionist, quirked an eyebrow as she reapplied her lipstick. "Let me guess, knocked up?"

"Bad food at lunch today." Refusing to rise to her bait, I joined her at the sink and calmly washed my hands. Katherine was one of those preppy girls, the kind who never had a hair out of place and wouldn't be caught in a morgue wearing anything other than a designer label. She also didn't hesitate to bare her claws if she thought someone was poaching on her turf. In her ice-blue eyes, Gage Channing was off-limits to everyone but herself.

Why couldn't he have chosen her to torment and terrorize?

I left the restroom, praying she wouldn't feed the office grapevine with stories of a pregnancy, and got stuck in rush-hour traffic on my way to BodyScape Spa, which proved to be a more humiliating experience than I imagined. Maybe it was because of Glenda's familiarity with "Mr. Channing's preferences," but I couldn't help but speculate on the number of women he'd sent there. Had there been others like me? Women he'd coerced and blackmailed? Or had they gone willingly? Gage was exceptionally attractive, and he was wealthy and successful to boot. A formidable package for sure, rolled into six feet of toned body, a head full of black hair, and a striking gaze that had the ability to pin you to the wall. I wasn't immune to how easy on the eyes my boss was.

For the past three years, I'd been immune to men period, and I'd certainly never entertained the idea of going to bed with my employer. It weirded me out to realize he'd been waiting for the perfect moment to ensnare me—to subject me to his twisted brand of sexual games.

"This'll hurt," Glenda warned. She ripped the wax off my leg like a Band-Aid, and I bit my lip to keep from groaning. I should be grateful it wasn't my bikini area; Gage had given Glenda instructions to leave me natural but trimmed down there.

The rest of the appointment went by much like the past hour had—in a daze. By the time I unlocked my car, night had fallen, and my nerves had multiplied. I wasn't ready for this. I didn't think twice about driving to the Hospital. I'd be late due to the detour, but I wasn't about to disappear on Eve without saying goodbye. Two days was a long time to a three-year-old.

Downtown Portland reflected a glittering skyline on the Willamette River, and Christmas lights lit up Pill Hill —which was home to the hospital. The temperature had dropped, and I was still rubbing my hands together when I arrived on Eve's floor.

"Good evening, Kayla," the nightshift nurse said. "Eve's been asking for you."

Guilt clawed at my gut. How could I expect my baby to understand? "Thanks, Mel." I headed to Eve's room, and her tiny face lit up the instant she saw me. Every day she grew paler, smaller—the hospital bed nearly swallowed her whole—but her eyes still sparkled with innocence.

"Hi, baby."

"Mama! Look what I color?" She proudly displayed her scribbled doodle.

"You drew this? You're so talented." I pulled her into a tight hug and held on a little longer than I normally would. The thought of being away for two days broke my heart. God, I was going to miss her. I blinked back tears and tucked her into bed. She jabbered on for a few minutes, words only a mother could detect without asking her to repeat them a dozen times.

"Eve," I began gently, "I've gotta go away—"

"Hello, Kayla."

My breath stalled at the sound of his voice. Time had

done nothing to erase it from my mind. I slowly turned. He stood in the doorway, a stethoscope dangling from his neck. God, he was a doctor now. Last I'd seen him, he'd been on the verge of entering medical school.

Last I'd seen him, I'd broken both of our hearts.

"Ian…it's been a long time." What kind of idiotic response was that? Seven years and that was all I could come up with?

His hazel gaze darted to Eve, and I didn't have to guess at the confusion on his face. Seven years ago I'd been pregnant; Eve was only three. "And apparently a lot has happened since." He brought a hand up and fiddled with the pen in his shirt pocket, and his eyes drifted to my left hand. Sometimes I still felt the phantom weight of my wedding band.

"You work here now?" I asked before he could voice the questions I saw in his eyes—the ones I didn't want to answer.

"Just transferred from Salem." He stepped inside and closed the door. "I heard your daughter was here. I wanted to come by and see you. See if I could do anything to help." He opened his mouth, then snapped it shut. "I'm sorry. I shouldn't have intruded like this."

"It's okay, you're not."

He moved to Eve's bedside. She'd settled into a light doze. "Leukemia?"

I wrapped my arms around myself and nodded.

"What phase is she?"

"Acute. She stopped responding to chemo."

"Jesus, Kayla." He ran a hand through his short hair;

it was lighter than I remembered. "I'm sorry."

"We're not giving up." I lost count of how many times I recited the phrase daily.

Ian was about to say more when my cell vibrated in my pocket. I pulled it out, and upon recognizing Gage's number, willed my face into a neutral mask. "I'm sorry, I have to go. I…I have a business trip this weekend. I tried getting out of it." I nibbled on my lip and looked at Eve. "I hate leaving her."

Ian pulled out a prescription tablet and wrote down his number. "Call me if you need anything. Or even if you don't…well, you know how to reach me now." His fingers brushed mine, lingering a few seconds as he passed me the slip of paper, and that familiar spark that had been dormant for so long sprung to life. My heart thundered in my ears as our eyes met. He started to move away, but I grabbed his arm.

"Ian, wait…there is something you can do for me." I let go of his sleeve. "Can you keep an eye on Eve for me? You know, if you're gonna be here?"

"That's not a problem. I can do that."

A lock of hair fell over his brow, and I clenched my fists to keep from brushing it back. "Thank you."

"No problem. I'll see you when you get back." He hesitated a few seconds, and then he noiselessly disappeared into the hall.

3. TRAINED

I barely remembered the drive to Gage's place in Portland Heights. My GPS directed me there, but if I needed to repeat the trip without assistance I'd more than likely get lost. A wall of trees cradled his massive house, affording a sense of seclusion even though the city sparkled below. Willing my skittish feet to stay put, I rapped on the door.

He yanked it open. "You're late." He took one look at my business suit and frowned. "Training you is going to be a challenge, I see." The corner of his mouth turned up, as if he relished the idea. Gage gestured for me to enter the foyer. He grabbed my purse before I could protest and rifled through it. "Hand over your phone, too."

"I need it in case the hospital calls."

"I've arranged for them to call me in case of an emergency."

Wondering how he'd managed that, I reluctantly handed him my cell. He also took my coat, and then he locked all of my belongings in a closet by the door. We stepped down into the living room. His home had been designed with a modern edge; vaulted ceilings, light oak flooring, and taupe walls that had surely never been victim to small, sticky fingerprints. His personality was stamped all over the sharp angles, the glass and steel.

I didn't get the grand tour. He ushered me to a door, which opened into a black hole of a basement.

"Where are you taking me?"

"You'll address me as Master when we're alone." He grabbed my chin and forced me to look at him. "Is that clear?"

"You're kidding, right?"

"No, I assure you, I am definitely not kidding, and the sooner you accept your place here, the easier it'll be on you. You've just arrived and already you've got two strikes against you, Kayla."

"For what?"

"Disobeying me. I told you to come naked, and you arrived late." He gestured for me to precede him down the stairs.

"I had to say goodbye to Eve. I couldn't disappear on her for the weekend without seeing her first." I grasped his arm to keep from stumbling. He flipped a switch, and the basement flooded with soft light.

The room was rectangular, dark and windowless, with deep crimson walls that matched the comforter on the king-sized bed; Gage had already laid several items on the end. A rack of cuffs, chains, whips, paddles, and God only knew what else hung on the far wall. An odd-looking bench sat in front of the display. Not certain what the X on the wall, the hooks in the floor and ceiling, or the plethora of items on the shelves were used for, I tore my gaze from the terrifying sight. A group of comfy chairs and a couch were arranged on a throw rug at the opposite end. Across from the bed a swanky bathroom, outfitted with a whirlpool tub and separate shower, could be seen through an archway.

Gage fisted my hair and yanked me against him. "These are my rules. Remember them." He trailed a hand down my throat, and his fingers settled on the buttons of my blouse. "Number one, don't fight me. If you do you'll be punished." He slowly unfastened each one, taking the time to brush his fingers against my skin. "Two, unless I've given you permission to speak freely, always call me Master when we're alone." He slid his hand inside and palmed my breast. "And three, obey without hesitation. Do you understand these rules?"

"I-I understand." I forced the words past my quivering lips.

He let out a low chuckle. "I don't think you do. I think it's time for your first punishment." He gripped my hair even tighter. "Before we go any further, you need to choose a safe word."

"And if I say this word…you'll stop?"

"Yes. And then I'll turn you over to the authorities. Neither of us wants that."

"Then what's the point in choosing a safe word? You know I won't use it."

"Because what happens here will be on my terms, but ultimately your choice. I won't move forward without it, so choose wisely, something you won't forget or accidentally say." He withdrew his hand from my breast and put a few inches between us. "It's the only word that will save you from your punishment. Screaming, crying, begging me to stop…none of those tactics will work."

"You sick bastard."

"You might consider showing me some respect—I'm the only person standing between you and a jail cell."

"Rick."

"Rick what?"

"Rick is my safe word."

"Who is Rick?"

I wrapped my arms around myself. "Someone I don't like to talk about."

"Answer the question. You'll withhold nothing from me."

"He's my ex-husband."

"An interesting choice for a safe word. Why'd you choose it?"

"Because I don't like to think about him, much less speak his name."

He whirled me around and curled his fingers around my wrists, then forced them to my sides. "Don't ever close yourself off to me again. I want your legs open and your arms at your sides. Always." He parted my blouse, and the material slid down my arms and floated to the floor.

Gage grabbed a thin strip of leather from the bed. "A collar to mark you as mine. It's discreet enough to wear in public. Don't take it off." He encircled my neck before reaching for a set of leather cuffs. "Give me your hands."

Instinctively, I shook my head. "Gage, what are you gonna do?"

His startling eyes pinned me. "I've been lenient. Until you agree to address me as Master, you'll not be allowed to speak." He grasped an odd ball contraption and mashed it against my lips. "Open your mouth."

Trepidation set in. "You don't need to do this. I'll call you Master."

"Yes you will. Now open your mouth." I feared the command in his tone, the underlying threat that if I didn't do as told, being gagged would be the least of my worries. I parted my lips, and the taste of rubber assaulted my tongue. He fastened the straps tight enough to make my jaw ache.

"Whenever your mouth is otherwise engaged"—his lips curved into a wicked grin, and I could only imagine what he was thinking—"you can snap your fingers in lieu of saying your safe word." He grabbed my hands and yanked them up, hooking them above my head. "Spread your legs."

My skirt bunched around my thighs as I obeyed, revealing a scrap of white panties. My pulse drummed in my ears, drowning out everything else as he kneeled down and fastened two more cuffs around my ankles. He placed a bar between them, ensuring I remained spread for him.

Gage stood and slowly pulled on a tether. "On your toes."

My eyes grew wide as he hoisted me up, and an unintelligible sound escaped me. The position made my breasts jut out and caused my legs to wobble until I was able to gain balance. I shifted my wrists, but they wouldn't budge. My arms and shoulders burned. How long was he going to make me stand like this? Better yet, what was he going to do?

I had my answer a moment later. He grabbed a pair of scissors and moved toward me. I panicked and let out a muffled cry as he came closer.

"Relax. I'm not going to hurt you. I want you naked." He slid the cool metal along my skin and cut away my bra, and tears overflowed as my breasts spilled free, right into the warmth of his waiting palms.

Gage fondled them, weighed them in his hands, and his gaze zeroed in on my hardened peaks. "Perfect, just the right size." He flicked his thumbs back and forth. I gasped for breath, vacillating between shame and arousal as every touch zinged to my core. Unable to take anymore, I tried to jerk away. He pinched each nipple and twisted, and I squeezed my eyes shut against the pain.

"Look at me, Kayla." He increased the pinch. I lifted my lashes and silently begged him to stop.

"You've got spirit, and you're stubborn. The more you resist, the more it turns me on." He released me and bent to his knees again. I couldn't stop trembling as he cut the skirt and panties from my body.

"You're so gorgeous strung up like that, helpless and open. Naked." His gaze journeyed over me, finally arriving at the juncture between my thighs. "Red indeed." He delved a finger inside, and I shot to the very tips of my toes.

"God, baby, you're so tight. How is that possible after giving birth?" His warm hand smoothed across my abdomen, and he traced the wounds left behind from my four years of marital hell. "What happened here?" The question was a rhetorical one, since I couldn't answer him verbally. "They look like knife wounds." He thrust another finger inside, gliding in and out, never breaking eye contact. I was helpless to do anything but accept his invasion. My eyes drifted shut.

"Don't." Another hard pinch of my nipple reminded me of his power. "I want you to watch me." With a twitch of a smile, Gage circled my clit with precision. My belly clenched, and I throbbed deep within as liquid heat ignited between my legs. "You're not allowed to hide your shame from me." He closed his mouth over a nipple and teased with his tongue, lightly nipped.

I squirmed as the fire in my body spread and intensified. God, it'd been so long. Too long. It was the only explanation for my reaction.

"You don't want to want me, but you do." He stroked me languidly, caressing in a sensual rhythm that drove me out of my mind. "I've been watching you, Kayla, noticing those shy glances you aim my way when you think no one's looking. If I didn't think this would work between us, I would've had you thrown in jail."

My muscles tightened, and I shamefully moved against his hand. I hadn't expected this, for him to make me want to come. A low moan escaped, and I almost did.

He pulled away abruptly. "You're not allowed to orgasm without my explicit permission. Like clothing, sexual gratification is a gift you must earn." He grabbed my chin and brought his face close to mine. "Take this time to think about your behavior."

Gage stepped away and smiled, as if we were conversing about something as mundane as the weather. His eyes wandered to my breasts, and my nipples begged for his touch, his mouth. "The room is under surveillance, so trust I'll keep an eye on you for safety reasons. I'm not a careless Master, but you must know where you stand with me. Disobedience will always earn you punishment. You'll stand like that for an hour."

An hour? I let out a pitiful cry.

He crossed his arms. "If you can't handle it, snap your fingers now."

Using my only way out wasn't an option, and we both knew it. Eve's pale face swam in my vision. I'd do anything for her. Anything. I shook my head, and by doing so gave him the okay. His heavy steps pounded the stairs, growing fainter the further he climbed. He was leaving! Oh God…an hour.

Fear enveloped me like a stifling blanket; an hour loomed ahead like eternity.

4. MASTERED

Time had no measure. Seconds, minutes…they all bled into each other until the only thing that mattered was the rampant ache in my muscles, the dimming of the room, the goose bumps forming on my skin as the chill set in. After a while I became numb. Listless. Found a place outside myself where I could tolerate existing. It was a familiar place, one I hadn't visited in a long time. I sagged toward the floor a little more with each minute, heels refusing to touch ground, wrists taking the burden of my weight.

And then I felt the warmth of his hands, grazing my ankles as he removed the bar from between my legs, circling my wrists and lifting…until they dropped like noodles at my sides. In a dizzying whirl, I slumped toward the floor. He engulfed me in his arms.

"Open your eyes, Kayla." His breath whisked across my face, tinted with brandy.

I stared into his sapphire gaze…and felt nothing.

He held me up with one hand and removed the gag

with the other. "Have you learned your lesson?"

I worked my aching jaw, and only then did I realize I had drool trailing down my chin.

"Answer me. Have you learned your lesson?"

"Yes."

"I'm giving you one chance, because I know your punishment wasn't easy. Show me the respect I'm owed."

My apathetic state diminished; swift anger welled and overflowed. I hated him. Truly despised him. "Go to hell, Gage."

He swept me up, threw me over his shoulder, and stalked to the bench.

"What are you doing?" I cried.

Ignoring my question, he dropped me to my feet. I grabbed onto the bench to keep from falling, which was a bad idea because my actions only helped him position me. Gage pressed onto my back and wedged my knees apart. He strapped my hands, knees, and ankles in place, and then he adjusted the bench until my butt tilted up for easy access.

The snap of leather sent ice through my blood. "What is that?" I cranked my neck around to see.

"A whip."

"Don't you dare hit me with that!" I couldn't breathe. Everything flooded back; the beatings, the bruises and cuts. The fractured bones.

"I told you what I expect from you, yet you continue to disobey me. If you can't take your punishment, say your word and end it." He punctuated his words with a swift strike to my ass.

I jerked and cried out, and the whip whistled through the air again, a split second warning before he struck me a second time.

Crack!

He hit me again and again, never giving me a moment to catch my breath, never allowing the sting to alleviate before he escalated the pain with another strike. I sobbed and pleaded with every blow, and eventually I found that place again—the place I'd lived in for the duration of my marriage.

Stop, stop, stop, stop…

Finally he did.

Tears drenched my face, and I couldn't see him, though the sound of his breath, coming fast and hard, told me he wasn't far. I ticked off the seconds in my mind and stopped counting when his legs came into view.

"Who am I, Kayla?"

I lifted my head. He still had a death grip on the whip; his knuckles had gone white around the handle. "You're my Master."

"That's right. Don't you forget it."

He put the whip away and then freed me from the restraints. "Don't move yet." He disappeared, only to reappear a few seconds later with a bottle of massage oil. He dripped some onto my back and went to work in rubbing the tension from my body. His fingers glided over my back and down my legs. I felt myself sinking, losing myself to the allure of my cloudy mind. Confusion niggled on the outskirts, and I vaguely wondered why he'd beat me only to massage away some of the pain afterward.

"Who am I?" His voice drifted above, rich and warm like hot chocolate. His hands chased the chills away from my skin.

"My Master," I mumbled.

He gripped my hand. "You can get up." Gage helped me to my feet and steadied me when I stumbled. "If you behave, I won't restrain you." He pointed to the bed. "Stand at the end and bend over the mattress." He reached for the button of his slacks.

The fog cleared, unveiling fear in its wake. "Please… Master…" I faltered. Would he be rough? Would it be quick?

"Do it now, Kayla."

My legs shook as I moved clumsily across the room. He pressed a hand against my back, and my breasts and stomach slid along the satiny comforter.

"Spread your legs."

On the verge of tears, I obeyed and opened for him. Chills traveled the length of my body; I couldn't stop shaking. I jumped when he grabbed my hips.

"Arms straight out in front of you." He massaged my sore ass. "Good, just like that. I want you to remain in this position, do you understand?"

I rested my cheek on the mattress as a tear escaped. "Yes, Master," my voice cracked, and I heard the distinctive slide of a zipper, the tear of a foil packet. For several seconds I waited, barely breathing, muscles tense in preparation for his intrusion.

He glided his fingers between my thighs. Keeping

perfectly still, I bit down on my lower lip. Unwelcome warmth flared again, and I prayed he'd stop caressing and just get it over with already.

"Please, Master, just do it."

"Oh, no, I'm not about to make this easy for you." He probed me with his fingers. "Do you know how many times I had to get myself off in my office after watching you prance around in your skirts?" He groaned. "You're getting wet, baby."

I arched my spine and bit back a moan.

"God, you're so responsive. I've wanted you for such a long time, wet and on the brink, begging for release." He plunged in, filling me with his pulsating heat, slowly stretching until I felt nothing but him.

I dug my fingernails into the bedding and closed my eyes in shame.

"If you come, I'll punish you." His breath fanned across my back. "Don't disobey me."

Yet the bastard took his time. I locked my jaw to keep quiet and trembled from the effort of holding back as he pumped in and out. I hated my body for betraying me.

It's only biology.

I held on to that thought as he pushed deeper. "You feel so good," he groaned. He increased his thrusts, exploiting a rhythm designed to send me spiraling out of control.

I fisted the comforter and unwittingly let out a long moan. "Master..."

"Don't come, Kayla."

I gritted my teeth and did the only thing I could think

of to cool the fire. I thought of Rick; replayed the day I escaped with Eve. I'd been two weeks postpartum when he'd beaten me in a drunken rage. Hours later, when I thought he'd finally passed out for the night, I'd grabbed Eve and hobbled toward the door. He'd come out of nowhere with the knife. Eve had been thrown into the corner, and I thanked God every day she hadn't been seriously hurt, though a broken arm had been serious enough.

After a while Gage tensed and shuddered, and I knew it was over. For now.

He withdrew and disposed of the condom "You've got impressive restraint. Not many women can hold back so well, not that they come here under your circumstances. I suspect that might have more to do with it. You feel forced."

My emotions were too close to the surface. On the heels of remembering in vivid detail how I'd escaped with my life—how Eve's future had depended on it—my rage exploded. I whirled around and pushed him. "That's because you did force me! Master," I bit out the last word as if it were poison. "You might be able to elicit a reaction from my body, but you'll never get the one you're truly after. You'll never have my eager participation." I took a step forward, emboldened by the stunned expression on his face. "It was easy to control myself. All I had to do was think of my ex-husband and how he nearly stabbed me to death."

Gage pressed his hand over my mouth. "I'd watch your tone. Don't villainize me—you're the one who stole ten grand. You signed the contract."

I pushed his hand away. "What you're doing is wrong, Gage. Punish me if you wish. Do your worst. You couldn't possibly hurt me more than he did." I turned my back on him, mostly because I figured it would piss him off.

I wasn't prepared for his laughter. "I do love a challenge. Sleep well, Kayla."

I hugged myself, and as his feet thumped up the stairs, I wanted to curl into a ball and cry myself to sleep. He shut the door, and the sound echoed through the basement, through the empty chamber of my heart.

5. INQUISITION

The following morning Gage ordered me into the bathtub. He sat on the edge, instructing me on how he expected me to bathe daily. The regimen he wanted me to follow would take a nice chunk out of my mornings, but I wasn't about to negotiate with him, not so long as the hard glint remained in his eyes. The new day had dawned with clarity; I'd gone too far the previous night. Now I had nothing to do but wait until he decided to dish out my punishment. My ass still stung from the one he'd given the night before—a constant reminder to call him "Master."

"I'm going to prepare breakfast. After you finish here, I expect you to wait on your knees until I return."

I gulped. "Why, Master?" I stood on the bathmat, tightly clutching the towel around my body. It didn't matter that he'd already seen me, had touched my most private places. I'd never be comfortable parading around naked in front of him.

"Because I ordered you to."

He left, and I waited until the echo of the door rang through the basement before I dried off. I took my time blow-drying my hair and applying makeup, but eventually I couldn't stall any longer. He still hadn't returned. With nothing else to do, I moved to the middle of the room and sank to my knees.

My thoughts drifted to Eve. I wondered what she was doing. Was she eating breakfast? I hoped they were able to get her to eat something. I also thought of Ian. Had he checked on her already? Suddenly, excitement fluttered in my stomach. If I behaved the way Gage wanted me to, took my punishment without complaint and sucked up to the bastard, maybe he'd let me call to check on her. I wondered if I'd get lucky enough to catch Ian at the hospital. Gage didn't have to know that "Dr. Kaplan" was more to me than a doctor.

I jumped as the door opened. He leisurely strolled down the stairs and stopped inches in front of me. He had no qualms about displaying the bulge behind his zipper. I looked up at him as dread squeezed my insides.

"I expect you to greet me on your knees from here on out. Understand?"

"Yes, Master," I answered automatically, though in reality I didn't understand any of it. How could anyone treat another human being this way? Maybe I was the damaged one and abusive men naturally flocked to me.

"Hungry?" he asked.

How did I answer that? My stomach growled, yet I feared he wasn't talking about food. "Yes, Master."

His mouth curved into a grin. "Seeing you on your

knees, calling me Master…" He rubbed himself. "Do you know what that does to me?"

"No, Master," I said, as if denying the evidence of his arousal would make it go away.

"You please me, Kayla. You've caught on quickly, faster than I thought you would."

I lowered my eyes.

"Look at me when I'm talking to you."

There was no mistaking the authority in his tone. I raised my eyes and didn't dare look away. Not with my ass still sore from the whipping he'd given me last night. Twenty-four hours hadn't passed and already I'd been reduced to a pathetic woman on my knees, my sole purpose to service and obey a man. Deep within, I silently screamed in rebellion and indignation. I hadn't hated myself this much since before my divorce.

He held out his hand, oblivious to my inner turmoil. "Come on, breakfast awaits."

I couldn't begin to describe my relief as I rose to my feet. Confronted with his arousal while on my knees made me ill. He led me upstairs, and I fought the urge to cover my breasts. I'd never walked around my own apartment naked, so the idea of walking around his home in the nude made me vulnerable on a whole new level. I suspected that was his intention.

We entered the dining room, and he dumped a bag of uncooked rice onto the hardwood floor next to the table. "Your punishment for getting mouthy with me last night." He pointed to the rice. "On your knees again."

I sank down, gritting my teeth as the grains dug into

my skin.

Gage sat in a chair and began feeding me fruit. He fed me breakfast bite-by-bite, and by the time he spooned up some yogurt, I wanted to slather my burning knees with it.

"I want to talk about your previous sexual experience." He fed me another spoonful of yogurt. "I'm going to ask you some questions," he continued, "and I want your complete honesty. Do you understand?"

"Yes, Master."

"Have you ever had anal sex?"

I lowered my head without thinking. What the question implied terrified me. I couldn't breathe.

"Kayla? I won't remind you again to look at me when I'm talking to you. Next time it happens, you'll be punished."

My gaze immediately shot to his.

He smiled. "That's better. Now answer the question."

"Once, Master," I said, my voice so low that he asked me to repeat myself.

"Did you like it?"

I shook my head, my throat constricting as the memories I'd worked so hard to bury burst through and flooded my mind.

"Why not?" He sounded genuinely curious.

"I-I...he forced me."

His face darkened. "And now you think I'm doing the same." It was a statement rather than a question.

I narrowed my eyes. "Because you are. You blackmailed me." I tempered my tone and added, "I had no choice, Master."

He rubbed the bridge of his nose and sighed. "I know I crossed a line with you, Kayla. I've had many women, and to be perfectly honest, they bored me. I want a woman who values self-respect, who is classy enough to refrain from bedding every man she meets. I wanted you."

I wanted to ask how I'd gotten so unlucky to be wanted by him, but remembering my hope to call the hospital, I bit my tongue.

He held out a hand. "You can get up now." I grabbed his hand and stood, and then I wiped the rice from my knees. Gage gestured toward the chair closest to him. "You can sit."

I sat down and didn't think twice about crossing my legs and arms. One look at his heated expression reminded me of his rules. I let my arms fall like noodles at my sides and uncrossed my legs, opening them several inches so he could see all of me.

He gave an imperceptible nod of approval and pushed my plate in front of me. "Finish eating. I have a few more questions."

I remained silent and bit into a piece of toast.

"How many men have you slept with?"

"Two, Master," I said, then immediately shook my head. "I mean three…since you…"

A smile teased his lips. "That's what I thought. I respect you for abstaining from the slutty behavior of most women. "Who were your lovers?

"My ex-husband and…"

Gage tapped his fingers on the table. "And?"

"A guy I knew in college, Master."

He frowned. "Sounds like there's more about this guy from college than you're letting on. Did you love him?"

"That's none of your business!"

His mouth flattened into a line, and I immediately regretted the outburst. "That's where you're wrong. If I say it's my business, then it is." He pushed his chair back and stood, and his hands bunched at his sides. "Were you in love with him?" There was no bend to his expression, no room for sympathy. Certainly no room for compromise. I was his, and he'd do with me as he pleased. Even if it meant making me answer what should have been a simple question.

"Yes, Master. I loved him." My rebellious nature rose, but I squashed it.

"Are you still in love with him?"

Oh shit. Would he believe me if I lied? Probably not. "It's been years, Master."

"That isn't what I asked. Answer the question, Kayla."

"Why does it matter to you?" *Smooth move, idiot. Keep pissing him off and he'll never give you access to a phone.*

He jerked a chair out from the table and sat. "Come here now."

I inched toward him. With swift agility, he reached out and pulled me over his knee.

My body tensed as his hand came down. "Are you in love with him?"

"Yes!" This punishment was more humiliating than painful.

"I want you to say 'I will not back talk my Master' after every swat of your ass."

Smack!

"I will not back talk my Master."

Smack!

I was wrong. Every strike of his hand grew more painful, and he didn't stop after just a few. He counted the spankings, his voice cool and mechanical. I was openly crying, struggling to recite the words with a semblance of coherency by the time he passed forty. He released me at fifty. "Sit down, Kayla."

I staggered back and eased into my chair with a wince.

"Don't test me again. You won't like the outcome." He picked up his coffee mug and took a sip. "Now, let's see if we can have a civilized conversation free of outbursts."

I was seething inside as I swiped the tears from my face. I scooped up a bite of yogurt before I lost my temper again.

"What is it about this man that has captured you so?"

I didn't know how to answer. It'd been so long since Ian had been a part of my life, and we'd barely had a chance before a surprise pregnancy had tipped my world upside down and I'd made the mistake of going back to my ex. That mistake had cost me my first baby. "I can't answer, Master. Not because I'm being difficult, but it's been seven years. A lot has happened. I don't know why there's still a part of me holding on."

"Did he satisfy you in bed?"

I felt my face grow warm. "Yes, Master."

Gage went silent for a few moments, and I took the opportunity to broach the subject of a phone call. "Can I ask you something, Master?"

He considered me carefully. "Go ahead."

"I'm worried about Eve. Would you…allow me the privilege of calling the hospital to check on her?"

"No."

I jumped out of my chair. "How can you be such a cold-hearted bastard?"

Displaying an irritating air of calm that nicked at my anger, Gage rose from his chair and crossed the dining room without a word. He halted in front of the tall hutch in the corner and withdrew something from a drawer. My stomach sank when I recognized the ball gag in his hands, similar to the one he'd used the previous night. He closed the distance between us and held it to my mouth. I clinched my jaw, displaying one last hint of fiery anger, and then parted my lips. Fighting him would only make things worse—I was beginning to understand this game he played.

Gage grabbed my hand and led me back to the basement. He took a seat in an overstuffed chair and pointed to the floor. I gave him a questioning look, as I wasn't sure what he wanted.

"I shouldn't have to spell it out for you, Kayla." He raised a brow. "You know your place by now, so stop being stubborn. Obey me."

I dropped to my knees.

"We'll discuss phone privileges another time, perhaps when you've found a way to rein in that mouth."

He didn't speak to me for the next hour. Drool trailed down my chin, dripped onto my breasts, and my knees ached and burned. He sat, a perfect picture of calm, reading a book while I suffered in silence. The stubborn part of me refused to give an inch. I wouldn't move, wouldn't shift and squirm or make a sound. I'd match him calm and raise him in strength any day.

6. FORBIDDEN RELEASE

Dinner went much more smoothly than breakfast. I managed to make it through the entire meal without a cross look from Gage or a punishment. Upon returning to the basement, he led me straight to the bench. My composure shattered.

"What are you doing, Master?" I resisted, which only caused him to firm his hold on me. "Why? What did I do?" I made him drag me across the room, thrashing the whole way.

"Knock this off right now!" He bent me over and spanked my ass. "Now crawl onto the bench before I issue a repeat of this morning."

I climbed up and got into position, and like the night before, he strapped me in. My body shook, from the chill in the room, from my absolute vulnerability. I jerked when his hands kneaded my ass.

"Don't hurt me, Master."

His hands smoothed up my back. "You need to learn to trust me. I won't punish you unless you deserve it.

Have you done anything to deserve it tonight?"

I hadn't thought so.

"Answer me."

"No, Master."

"This isn't about punishment." He swept my hair to the side and trailed his fingers down my spine. "We're going to explore anal play," he said. "I don't want this to be traumatic for you, so we'll ease into it by using a butt plug, but eventually I want to fuck your ass."

"Don't do this." My voice broke.

"If you want me to stop, you have the power in one little word, Kayla."

I whimpered as he spread my cheeks. Oh God, it was going to hurt. He was bigger than my ex, and when Rick had forced himself into that tight space, I hadn't been able to sit down for days. I'd been a week postpartum, and he hadn't wanted to wait for me to heal after giving birth.

He moved away and opened a cupboard. When he returned, his cool hands slid over my butt again. I felt trapped, absolutely helpless. I could do nothing to stop him, short of saying the word that would void our contract. We both knew that wasn't going to happen. A squirting sound broke the utter quiet in the basement, and Gage applied a cold, jelly-like substance.

I automatically tensed as he dipped a finger inside

"How does that feel?" he asked.

I gritted my teeth. "It burns, Master."

"Relax your ass."

I willed my mind past the pain and concentrated on

releasing the tension in my body.

"Better?" he asked.

Surprisingly, it was. "Yes."

He used his fingers for a while before introducing the butt plug. "You need to stay relaxed. If you don't it'll only hurt more."

"Please, Master, don't. I'm not ready for this."

"Yes, you are. You're only fighting it because you're scared. I won't hurt you, but you've gotta loosen up." He slowly inched in the plug, and I let out a screeching cry.

"Stop," I sobbed. "Please…stop." I fought against the restraints until the leather cuffs bit into my tender skin.

"Relax your muscles," he said again. The pressure in my rectum increased as he shoved it all the way in. He reached between my legs and circled my clit. "Let your body adjust to it." Something about the husky quality of his voice caused tingles to spread through me; I was stunned to find myself aroused.

What the hell was this man doing to me?

"How does it feel now?"

I wet my lips and tasted the salt of my tears. "Weird, Master."

"Does it still hurt?"

"A little." Not like it had when my ex had forced his way in there. Maybe the difference lie in the preparation.

He crawled onto the bench and straddled me from behind, and I heard him unzip his pants. Gage pressed against my back and whispered directly into my ear, "Are you turned on?"

"Yes, Master." Humiliation washed over me.

"Do you want me to fuck you?"

I gave him the answer he wanted to hear. "Yes, Master."

Before I could take my next breath, he thrust into me. I was already wet and ready for him. The pressure from the butt plug heightened the pleasure, making each plunge a sensation that drove me closer to losing control. I moved with him as he pumped in and out, no longer caring if I was acting like a desperate hussy. The need inside me clawed to the surface; I could deny it no longer. I was on the verge of release, breaths coming in gasping pants, when he painfully fisted my hair.

"Not yet, baby. Not until I give you permission."

"Gage!" I cried out again, barely managing to rein in my orgasm. "I can't, Master!"

He groaned. "Yes you can."

I dug my fingernails into the leather of the bench, groaning as the pressure built to the erupting point. "Please, Master…please…"

He shot upright onto his knees and smacked my ass. "Not yet."

I let out a scream as the violent orgasm tore through my body. "Oh God!" I arched my back, curled my feet, and wondered if the wave would ever end.

Gage came then, releasing a hoarse cry that caused my insides to clench all over again.

"I couldn't stop it, Master."

"You know I'll have to punish you for that, right?"

Gasping for breath, I let my head fall to the bench and nodded. At the moment I didn't care. I'd never experienced such an intense orgasm. Ever. I closed my eyes, my heart still pounding a fast beat, and allowed the overwhelming surge of emotion to spill over.

7. VULNERABLE

As part of my slave duties, Gage assigned me a list of chores Sunday morning. After I'd done the dishes, folded his laundry, and vacuumed, he reinserted the butt plug and ordered me to scrub both of his bathrooms on my hands and knees.

Only his idea of clean surpassed mine by a hundred miles. He'd made me redo my first attempt, instructing me to use a toothbrush. I'd since moved on to the bathroom in the basement and was now scrubbing the grout between the tiles with a vengeance, all the while silently cursing him.

"R" is for rotten scoundrel.

"S" is for Satan.

"T" is for—

I gasped as the pressure in my ass shifted—it had been there for so long, I'd begun to get used to it. I stilled as he teased me by sliding the plug out a couple of inches, only to push it back in. I couldn't decide if I liked the sensation or not. He did it again, and I unconsciously raised my ass.

"You like that, huh?" He dipped his fingers between my legs, and the toothbrush fell from my hand and clattered to the floor.

I moaned with each thrust, with every motion of his fingers. I didn't recognize the woman I'd become; on hands and knees on a bathroom floor, coming undone as my boss fucked me in the ass with a butt plug.

Gage pulled away. "Get up."

I obeyed and slowly turned to look at him. He was completely naked. Warmth flushed my cheeks. Ashamed of what he'd reduced me to, I had a difficult time meeting his gaze.

He pulled me against him. "You need a shower, and I need you to take care of this." He grabbed my hand and closed my fingers around his erection. I stroked him as he backed me toward the stall. Gage guided me inside and switched on the shower. Hot water cascaded over us, coming from all directions from the multiple shower heads.

He pushed my back against the wall. "Hold on to these," he said, lifting my arms and folding my fingers around the two handles built into the shower stall. "Close your eyes. I want you to feel every touch, every sensation."

My eyes drifted shut, and his soapy hands glided over my skin, fingers teasing breasts, smoothing down my stomach, caressing between my thighs. He left no area untouched. My pulse fluttered at my throat, and when he laved his tongue there, I arched my neck and let out a sigh.

"You're so beautiful," he whispered against my skin. "So responsive to my touch."

The warmth of his mouth closed around a nipple. I whimpered, overcome with need, and tightened my grip on the handles. The way he set me off reminded me of the night I'd spent with Ian all those years ago. I hadn't experienced such intense desire in years; my ex had surely never made my body hum.

Gage grabbed my ass and hoisted me against him. "Wrap your legs around me," he said. "Keep your eyes closed."

I obeyed his command. He ran his hands up my back and burrowed them in my hair. I parted my lips and tasted water as it streamed down my face. His mouth came down on mine, and my mind fogged over as his tongue swept inside. His kiss was sensual, urgent, possessive, and erotic, all rolled into one. He kissed like he smiled—with a devilish edge that was too tempting to ignore. He delved deeper, and I lost my mind as he thoroughly possessed my mouth. For a few blissful minutes, I forgot how he'd forced me there, forgot about the beating, the humiliation. For the first time in years, I felt alive.

He broke away, and without thinking, I opened my eyes; I'd never seen his so bright. In that moment I saw him for the first time. Really saw him, his face softened in vulnerability.

"Turn around," he said hoarsely.

Limbs shaking, I did as I was told.

"Grab the handles and climb up."

I looked down and noticed the built-in seat, made specifically to accommodate a woman's knees. I got into position, and Gage ran his fingers down my spine. He palmed my ass and then dipped the plug in and out.

"Master…" I moaned and arched my back.

"Yes, baby, just like that. You're gorgeous in this position." He lightly spanked me. I jumped, not because it hurt, but because the slap was so unexpected. He slapped my ass again, and then he spread my cheeks.

My heart thundered in my ears as he removed the plug and applied lubricant. Apprehension twisted my insides.

"Hold on to those handles," he said.

Gage's thick cock slowly pressed in. His intrusion stretched me further, and I gasped for breath at the intensity of the burn, clamped my fingers around the handles, and focused on breathing. I now knew how pleasurable it could feel if I let my mind and body accept it.

"How does it feel?"

"It burns, Master."

"Try to relax." He pushed in another inch.

"I can't!" My knuckles turned white. "Stop—"

"Relax your muscles, Kayla. I'm not trying to hurt you." He groaned softly against my ear. "I'm being as gentle as I can, but if you can't loosen up you'll have to endure the pain. This won't be the last time I fuck you like this." He took his time, easing in a little more with each thrust. My knees trembled, and Gage wound his arms around me and palmed my breasts, supporting me with his strength. He sipped at the water sluicing down my neck and dove deeper. "You feel so good."

I squeezed my eyes shut, and after a while my body grew accustomed to his. With a final jerk, he came and collapsed onto my back. We stayed frozen like that for a while, me relieved it was over, and him coming down from the high he'd achieved.

He got up and shut off the water. "Come on," he said, gently tugging on my arm. I got to my feet. We dried off with fluffy towels, and he ushered me into the basement. I eyed the bench, remembering my forbidden orgasm from the day before, and wondered if he planned to strap me onto it and beat me again.

But he bypassed the bench and headed for the bed. "Have you been wondering how I'm going to punish you?"

I bit my lip and nodded.

He crawled onto the mattress and sat with his back to the headboard. He patted his lap. "Come here."

I blinked. "Do-do you want me to straddle you, Master?"

"No, I want you to sit facing away."

I hesitated a second before climbing onto the bed. The friction of my skin sliding along his excited me.

"Lie against me."

I reclined against his chest. Gage wedged his legs between mine and spread my thighs.

"I want you to touch yourself until you reach the point where you're about to orgasm, then I want you to stop. If you come, there will be consequences."

I swallowed hard. I'd never gotten myself off before in front of another person, and I'd certainly never had to hold back. With tentative fingers, I reached down and stroked myself, slowly rubbing in a way that was familiar and sensual. Yet the usual build-up was absent. I squirmed and tried to force myself into the right mindset, but after several minutes my breathing was still too even, the tingles in my body too weak.

He kissed the hollow of my shoulder. "Close your eyes," he whispered, "do whatever you have to, but get yourself to the edge. You're not stopping until you do."

I inhaled a deep breath, closed my eyes, and turned my mind off to anything but the feel of his warm skin underneath me, the zinging sensation deep in my stomach as his hands brushed across my breasts. My center liquefied as my fingers circled with increasing speed. A blissful ache rushed through my limbs, and my heartbeat reached a thundering roar. I jerked my hand away. My chest heaved in his hands, and I panted and squirmed, hating how the ache lingered between my legs.

Gage's own breathing had grown heavy. Just as the pressure started to subside, he pushed my hand back to my crotch. "Do it again, and stop before you come."

I tunneled my fingers through my slick folds, and my body immediately responded. He made me rub myself to the edge several times, until I was openly moaning and grinding my butt against his erection. Blood rushed through me, molten lava coalescing at the epicenter between my legs. On the brink of exploding, I trembled so violently that my legs cramped. He whisked his thumbs across my nipples and I almost burst into flames.

"Please," I groaned. "I can't…"

He trapped my hands in his. "Control it. Hold it in. You don't have my permission to come."

I arched and dug my fingernails into his skin. Several minutes passed in silence, and when he pushed my hand back to the center of all that throbbing heat, I thought I'd die. He forced me to the edge one last time, and then he slid from the bed and fastened my hands to the headboard. "Wouldn't want you to give in to temptation," he said with a crooked grin. "I'll be back in an hour. Hopefully you'll have calmed down by then."

8. HOME

As a reward for my iron-like control over my body, Gage took me out to dinner that night. After existing in a naked state for two days, I found the sensation of clothing against my skin wonderful. Now I almost felt normal, seated like a lady, surrounded by fashionable people at a fancy restaurant with an attractive man smiling back at me from across the table.

Almost.

Beyond the surface, nothing about the situation was normal, especially since the man in question had inserted a butt plug in my ass before we'd left the house. I recrossed my legs for the fifth time and tried not to squirm.

"You're gorgeous. I'm a lucky man to be accompanied by the most beautiful woman in the restaurant."

Luck had nothing to do with it, but I kept my thoughts to myself. I'd managed to get through the rest of the day without further punishment or pain, if you didn't count the pulsing ache between my thighs that refused to subside. He'd given me more chores to complete and had come to me for sex twice already. I hadn't been allowed to orgasm; as a result I was tense with sexual frustration.

He lowered his gaze to my breasts and smiled in amusement. "Still feeling a little uncomfortable?"

I clenched my jaw. My nipples had been hard pebbles of need for most of the evening. I felt them poking out now.

"Answer me, Kayla." Even in public, he didn't hesitate to wield his authority over me.

"Yes, Mast—" I broke off, remembering that I wasn't supposed to call him Master in public. "I'm sorry. Yes, I'm "uncomfortable."" That was one way of putting it.

The waiter arrived at our table. He was young, maybe a couple years younger than my twenty-eight years. He flashed a boyish grin at me, and Gage's expression darkened.

"Good evening," he said, "we have several specials on the menu tonight. Can I interest you in a bottle of wine?" He directed the question at Gage and then took a small step back at the dangerous look in his eyes.

"A bottle of Pinot Grigio, please."

The waiter scurried away, and Gage blasted me with his granite expression. "Don't look at him when he returns. I'll order for you."

I lowered my gaze. *Just bite your tongue. The weekend's almost over, just get through it.*

The waiter returned a few minutes later, and in my peripheral vision I saw him present a bottle. Gage went through the whole swirl and taste routine and gave a nod. Wine swished into my glass an instant later, and the waiter left after taking our orders.

"Are you going to visit Eve tonight?" Gage asked.

"Yes. I'm sure she's missing me."

An uncomfortable silence settled over us. How odd that he had nothing more to say to me, considering he knew my body inside and out by now. When the food arrived, I kept my eyes on my hands. The meal went by painfully slow, filled with long silences and small talk that was unnatural and awkward. It was as if the two of us didn't know how to operate together outside of the office or the bedroom.

Gage had shaken up my world with a new dynamic: I didn't know how to act around him anymore. Would things be this tense at the office?

I let out a sigh of relief when we returned to his house. At least there I knew where I stood. He'd trained me well over the weekend, had made it clear where my place was; on my knees at his feet. He shut the door, and as soon as I shed my coat, he picked me up and pressed me against the wall. His fingers tore through nylon, shoved aside panties, and his cock slammed into me before I could catch my breath. He pulled the butt plug out, and I heard it drop to the floor.

It was, perhaps, our shortest session yet. After climaxing, he zipped up and walked into the living room without a word.

"Did I do something wrong, Master?"

"No." He grabbed a notebook from the coffee table

and turned to me. "I want you to remember who you belong to. I don't take kindly to other men undressing you with their eyes."

He was blowing it out of proportion—the guy had only smiled at me—but I wasn't about to argue with him.

"Before you go, we need to discuss a few things." He handed me the notebook. "It's a journal, and on the first page you'll find a list of rules. Also included are my expectations outlining what you should eat and wear during the week. I want you to write in the journal every night. List what you did during the day, who you saw, what you ate and wore, and I especially want you to list any rules you broke."

I took the notebook from him. Despite his demands, a sense of freedom awaited me through that door, even if the next five days would go by too fast. God, how I was going to hate the end of each day, bringing me that much closer to next weekend.

"Can I go now, Master?"

"Yes. I'll see you tomorrow morning at the office."

I shrugged into my coat, concealing the torn state of my nylons, and opened the door. Gage's hand shot out and blocked my exit.

"Kayla—" He grabbed the back of my head and brought my mouth to his. The kiss went on for what seemed like forever. By the time he broke away, my pulse pounded in my ears. "If you disobey me, I *will* find out. Don't forget you're mine."

I averted my eyes, and he jerked my face back to his. "Do you understand?"

"Yes, Master." I stepped outside and shivered; I wasn't entirely certain the chill was from the weather. The next five days promised blessed freedom. Time spent with Eve, maybe even a few forbidden moments at the hospital with Ian. I planned to make every one of them count.

9. THE RULES

Whoever said crying was a form of cleansing hadn't cried over the shit I had in my lifetime, the most recent of which took the cake—namely that my daughter was fighting for her life. I'd stolen from the devil himself in order to save her, and now I was paying the ultimate price: six weeks of forced slavery of the most vile variety.

The fact that a part of me enjoyed it only compounded the problem.

I unlocked my door and finally allowed the floodgates to break. I'd barely kept my tears at bay while at the hospital, where I'd pulled Eve into my arms and rocked her long after she'd fallen asleep. I wasn't sure if I'd held on so long to comfort her or me, but the weight of her in my arms and the smell of her soft skin had righted my world, if only for a while. I'd needed someone in that moment, and sadly I had no one but my three-year-old daughter.

I shed my clothes and collapsed into bed, and the sense of safety I usually felt within these walls was absent.

Gage Channing's lingering intrusion permeated every corner of my sanctuary. I curled into a ball and hugged my naked body, letting it all out in gulping sobs. The rest of the night blurred—hours blending together as the clock on my nightstand moved time...moved time closer to when I'd have to see him again.

Confusion and grief were powerful emotions; they haunted me now as heavily as my guilt did—the most disturbing case imaginable. I tortured myself with the vivid memory of his sculpted body moving against mine, demanding my submission, and his whip lancing my bare skin in unforgiving blows. Worse was how he'd forced me to pleasure...how even now I craved it.

I still ached from being denied so long. Despite his damn rules, I slid my hand between my thighs and closed my eyes, burrowing my fingers into slick, throbbing heat. My frenzied touch brought me to an exquisite build-up. Gage's blue-eyed gaze flashed in my head, and as I recalled the experience of grinding against him—again and again without release—I plunged into inevitable rapture, coming long and hard. A deep moan poured from my throat, and I spread my legs wider as my body cramped and shuddered. Heart pounding a deafening rhythm, I gave over to my release as it pulsed around my fingers. A blessed haze engulfed me, and I drifted to sleep a couple hours before the sun peeked through the blinds.

The blaring alarm interrupted an alternate replay of Gage and me in my dreams. There had been no cruelty, no hunger for power and dominance—he'd touched me with the gentlest patience and whispered the sweetest words, unlike the language he'd used over the weekend.

I want to fuck your ass.

Yes, dream-Gage had been ten times better than foul-mouthed, sadistic Gage with his demands and a whip to ensure I bowed to him. I got to my feet and began his mandatory hygiene regimen.

Bath oil in the water—check.

Wash and condition hair—check.

Shave underarms, bikini area, and legs from thigh to ankle—check.

Rub jasmine scented lotion over every inch of skin—check.

I'd have to stop by the department store on my way to work to pick up a pair of four-inch heels—another requirement. He even demanded I wear them to the hospital and while running errands. With a sigh, I ransacked my closet in search of a short skirt. A deep forage into my lingerie drawer produced a lacy bra and thong set I'd forgotten about long ago. I hadn't worn such things in…

Shit, I couldn't remember the last time I'd worn something so sexy. If Gage hadn't promised to set up an account for me at Victoria's Secret, I'd be in real trouble. As I moved toward the kitchen to turn on the coffee maker, a drift of cool air hit my ass. I hated thongs.

I hated Gage Channing even more.

I picked up the journal he'd given me and re-read his "rules…"

No masturbating.

Oops, already broke that one.

No dating, flirting, or touching/having sex with other men. No talking to men, unless work, errands, or hospital personnel require it.

Not likely to happen, since my social life was non-existent. A niggling thought bothered me. Ian might fall into this category. I couldn't help my feelings for him, years ago buried but never forgotten, and I couldn't help if I ran into him at the hospital. What was I supposed to tell him? That I wasn't allowed to speak to him? Yeah, as if that wouldn't raise a few questions, not to mention an eyebrow or two.

Must maintain hygiene regimen daily.

I already despised this rule.

Must always wear the collar.

The damn thing choked me, if not literally then figuratively. The thin strip of leather was a constant reminder that no matter how close freedom seemed within my grasp, it truly wasn't.

Must follow the specified menu plan.

This one could be a problem, since most days I didn't have an appetite at all.

Must wear four-inch heels, short skirts, and thong underwear at all times (work, hospital, errands).

Perverted bastard.

Must sleep naked.

Ditto.

10. OFFICE PUNISHMENT

I was shaking by the time I exited the elevator, anxious and terrified of facing Gage again after what had happened between us over the weekend. The office bustled with the normal Monday morning activity I'd become accustomed to during my employment at Channing Enterprises. Katherine gave me her patented sugary smile as I stumbled toward Gage's office in my new heels. I cursed the squished nature of my toes, and then cursed again when some of his coffee splashed onto my hand. Already on the verge of being late, I licked up the bitter liquid and hoped no one noticed. The caffeine went straight to the butterflies in my stomach; they fluttered with the energy of a crack addict. I knocked on his door and pushed it open upon his order to enter.

He sat behind his desk, a phone wedged between his ear and shoulder as he entered data into his laptop. He didn't acknowledge me as I set down the coffee cup with a trembling hand. I pulled my iPad from my briefcase and shuffled my feet as he finished the call.

"Good morning, Kayla." He grabbed the cardboard cup and took a sip before going about his normal morning routine, which involved dictating what he needed me to do for him. My fingers flew over the screen, adding meetings, notes, and anything else he specified. He said nothing remotely related to our weekend together—not even a hint. He resumed typing, and I kept my mouth shut, though I had to admit to being completely flustered. He acted as if nothing out of the ordinary had happened. I couldn't help but stand there like an idiot, waiting for some sort of response— something to indicate how I should behave around him. Was I supposed to call him Master while in his office when no one else was around? Did he want me on my knees as long as the door was closed?

I cleared my throat. "Mr. Channing?" Uttering that name left an odd taste in my mouth after the weekend I'd endured. Not only had he effectively programmed me to call him "Master," but addressing him so formally after he'd had his cock buried in me seemed ridiculous. I licked my lips, thinking of the one place he had yet to penetrate. I'd be naive to assume it wasn't going to happen eventually.

He glanced up. "Yes?"

"Is there anything else?"

"No, that's all. I'll need that report by lunch." He returned to his work, and I didn't know what confused me more—his casual dismissal, or the fact that it stung.

I put Gage's behavior out of my mind and got to work. Shortly before lunchtime, as I was gathering a printout, Tom from the marketing department approached me.

"How was your weekend?" he asked.

I blinked. "It was…nothing unusual. How was yours?"

"Could've been better. Cindy and I broke up."

"I'm sorry."

"Don't be. It was a long time coming. Actually, I wanted to ask you out for coffee. You busy this week?" He took a step closer and brushed a stray hair out of my eyes. "Or we could do something more private. Whatever you're up for."

I gave him an uneasy smile. "I'm sorry, I can't. My daughter's in the hospital." I stumbled back until a couple of feet separated us.

Apparently he didn't pick up on my subtle hint. "How's she doing?" he asked, closing the distance.

"Her doctor's hopeful. We're waiting on some test results." I looked toward Gage's office and found his thunderous expression aimed in our direction. He crossed the space with a purposeful stride.

Oh, shit.

"You're fired," he snapped at Tom. "Security will escort you from the premises." Gage gave a slight nod toward a man who materialized from the periphery. He grabbed Tom by the arm.

"What the hell?" Tom's eyes widened as he took in our employer's furious expression. "Why? What'd I do?"

"I won't tolerate sexual advances between my employees. You obviously made Ms. Sutton very uncomfortable."

"Let's go," the security guard ordered.

Tom protested, his voice ringing through the fifth floor as the guard escorted him to the elevator. "I'll have you sued for this!" As soon as they disappeared behind the sliding doors and all the prying eyes pretended to go back to work, I set my hands on my hips and glared at Gage.

"Was that really necessary? He has a kid to take care of!" I wasn't sure who was more surprised by my outburst —him or me.

"In my office *now*."

I closed my eyes on an exhale. Once again I'd let my mouth run rampant. Every gaze in the room weighed on me as I trailed behind Gage. He shut and locked the door, and I swallowed hard, preparing to grovel.

"I'm sorry. I was way out of line."

He grabbed my arm and yanked me over to his desk. There wasn't much on it—a few papers, a stapler, and the coffee cup from this morning. He swept everything to the floor, and black coffee splashed the wall.

"How dare you disrespect me in front of my employees. It's bad enough I had to watch that idiot manhandle you."

"You're right. I was wrong to question you in front of everyone."

"Has one night of freedom erased your training already? You will address me as Master, and so we're clear, you were wrong to question me at all." He unbuckled his belt and gestured to the desk. "Bend over."

I didn't dare hesitate. If I did as told, maybe he would go easy on me.

"Lift up your skirt. If you drop it, I'll make your hands bleed."

With shaking fingers, I lifted the back of my skirt and exposed my bare bottom.

"You've brought this on yourself, Kayla." The slide of his belt shattered the quiet as he removed it. "If you ever let another man touch you again, I'll do far worse." The strap of leather came down hard enough to steal my breath.

I blinked back tears, knowing that leaving his office with blotchy eyes and streaking mascara was more humiliation than I could stand. I pressed into the desk to brace myself and gripped my skirt tighter in preparation for the next blow.

"How many strikes do you think you deserve?"

Was he fucking serious? How could I answer without getting ensnared in his trap?

"As many as you see fit, Master."

"Very diplomatic answer. That's one thing I like about you—you're a smart woman."

Crack! I jumped at the stinging bite. Holy hell it hurt.

"Do you think I enjoy this, Kayla?"

"Yes, Master," I choked out.

"You'd be wrong." He struck me again, and I couldn't hold back a sob. I squeezed my eyes shut, but it did little to shut out the pain. "I won't deny that the sound of your cries, the display of your submission and vulnerability, gets me hard, but I'd much rather get past the need to punish you at all." The belt whooshed through the air again, and I bit into my lip as it connected with my tender skin.

He stopped at ten. "Come here."

I turned around in time to see him drop the belt. Upon my hesitation, he flexed his hands. Slowly, I crossed the three feet that separated us, my skirt swishing against my burning ass as I moved. He reached out and gripped my shoulders, pushing down until I was kneeling before him. The hard ridge behind his zipper stared me in the face.

Gage unbuttoned his slacks, and the slight tremble in his hands didn't go unnoticed; he was worked up, though from anger or desire, I couldn't be sure. "Unzip me."

I raised my head, though I knew my silent pleading wouldn't do any good.

"Don't look at me like that. You're only going to piss me off more."

"Please, Master—"

"I want my cock in your mouth *now*."

Holding back another sob, I pulled down his zipper, and his shaft popped out, hard and ready for my lips and tongue.

He fisted my hair with both hands and held me in place.

"Don't make me do this, Master. Please, not here."

His cock twitched. "Beg some more. It turns me on."

I clenched my jaw. I wondered what he'd do if I refused? Did I want to find out?

No, I didn't.

Several seconds went by, during which neither of us moved. He was waiting for me to take the initiative, and I was waiting for him to force me. It would be easier if he did. Every inch I gave him felt like a betrayal to myself. He tickled my mouth with the tip, bathing my lips with his desire. He'd win this standoff; I'd lost the game before I even knew how to play.

I darted my tongue out to taste him. More moisture collected at the head, and his salty taste lingered on my tongue. It'd been years since I'd given a blow job, but I was pretty sure I still remembered how. I reached out and fisted the base, and then teased him with my lips, swirling a wet path around the soft tip a few times before fastening my mouth around him.

Gage expelled a deep moan, and his grip on my hair tightened to an unbearable pull. The fact that his response tingled between my legs shouldn't have shocked me by now, but it did. And it shamed me. A part of me got off on the power I had in this moment. He might have forced me to my knees, but I could bring him to his with the heat of my mouth, the kiss of my tongue. I took him in as far as I could stand and worked him for all I was worth.

His choppy breathing infused the air, and he began to thrust, forcing my head back with each forward motion. Pumping in and out, deeper, faster, keeping time to the friction of my mouth and hands. His gaze intensified, and unsettled with how he watched me, I closed my eyes.

"Look at me," he ordered on a groan. I met his glazed-over eyes as he jerked to the back of my throat.

His taste flooded my mouth, and when I tried to pull away, he immobilized me in his grasp. I couldn't keep from gagging as his cum shot down my throat. The way he tightened his fingers, pulling against my tender scalp, told me he enjoyed making me gag as much as he enjoyed spilling into my mouth.

He withdrew, zipped up with casual patience, and then indicated the spilt coffee on the floor—the evidence of his rage and jealousy. "Clean this up before you go to lunch. I have a meeting I'm late for." He picked up his belt and looped it through his pants, and just like that the bastard left me kneeling in the middle of his office, wet between my thighs as his cum dribbled down my chin.

I got up on jittery legs and stumbled to his private bathroom. A few splashes of cold water to my face, followed by the mindless task of cleaning up after his fit, helped me find composure. When I left his office, grabbing a file folder on the way to make it look like I'd had legitimate business in there, I did my best to appear unfrazzled. I cringed to think of the office grapevine catching wind of what Gage had forced me to do.

My lunch hour passed much too quickly, and upon my return I managed to avoid my coworkers and Gage for the duration of the day by hiding away with a laptop in a vacant windowless office. Privacy was a must, since I couldn't sit without grimacing. I was unprepared for the whispers and incredulous looks as I gathered my briefcase and purse at the end of the day.

One glance into Gage's office revealed it was empty. He was either away at a late meeting, or he'd already left. I stiffened when someone whispered the word "slut" as I made the long journey toward the elevator. From the corner of my eye I recognized Katherine. She laughed, her blond head bent close to someone else's. They both snickered, and I felt their eyes bore holes into my back. I was content to ignore them until I heard the term "blow job" drift through the office.

Rage and mortification collided in my chest, and I hardly breathed as I sought refuge behind the elevator doors. I blinked, silently repeating *I will not cry* over and over again as the elevator descended. If everyone knew what had happened today in Gage's office, then he must have told someone. Barreling out into the pounding rain, I was thankful for Oregon's weather as the raindrops disguised my tears. I slid into the privacy of my car and pulled out my cell.

Gage answered on the third ring. "This better be important."

"You're damn right it's important!" I dashed the tears from my face and lowered my voice. "Everyone knows." God, how was I going to keep this job now? It was difficult enough to envision working for the devil himself after entering into a contract with him, but to withstand the ridicule of his employees…and not be able to defend myself with the truth…I couldn't do it. Yet I had no choice. The pay was too good, and even with Gage covering Eve's medical bills, I was still entrenched in debt. I couldn't afford to change jobs.

I heard him speak to someone else, and then the distinctive sound of a door closing filtered to my ear.

"What are you talking about, Kayla?"

"They called me a slut, and someone mentioned 'blow job.' How could you tell anyone? Haven't you tortured me enough?"

"First off, watch your tone. Don't forget who you're speaking to. Secondly, I don't flaunt my business, so I have no idea what you're talking about."

"Someone found out. They know what happened today in your office."

He let out a heavy sigh. "I need to finish up here. Are you on the way to the hospital?"

"Yeah."

"Are you alone right now?"

"I'm in my car."

"Then why aren't you addressing me as Master? This changes nothing. You'll be punished for your lack of protocol tonight. Come to my house at nine."

A violent shudder tore through me. Freedom didn't exist within Gage's contract—I wouldn't be free for another five and half weeks. Like a trained dog, I replied, "Yes, Master."

A small part of me wondered if I'd ever be free of him.

11. FROM BAD TO WORSE

The hair on the back of my neck stood on end as I rushed through the rain toward the hospital. The uneasy sensation of being watched settled over me, though in the back of my mind I knew the feeling was likely a result of what had happened in the office earlier. I felt exposed and on display, as if every person I crossed paths with thought the word "slut" after a single glance.

The instant I entered Eve's room, my paranoid worry about gossip and rumors vanished. Dr. Leah Gordon's weary expression threatened to strangle me. My heart plummeted, and I instinctively sensed something was wrong.

"Kayla, maybe you should have a seat."

I shook my head. "No, just tell me."

Her shoulders slumped slightly. "Eve's blood work came in. It's not encouraging."

"But...but..." I suddenly couldn't form a coherent sentence. The walls in the room closed in as the doctor's words percolated in my head. "You said her chances were good…"

Dr. Gordon laid a comforting hand on my shoulder. "I was optimistic, yes, but we're not seeing the results I'd hoped for."

I brought a trembling hand to my mouth. Eve was fast asleep in bed, her skin so pale it nearly matched the pasty color of the bed sheets. My eyes zeroed in on the dried blood caking the skin underneath her nostrils. "She had another nose bleed?"

"Yes, and she became quite agitated. The nurse got her to calm down by rocking her. She's been resting for the past hour."

I grabbed a washcloth and ran it under warm water, then gently wiped her face. She stirred but didn't wake. She looked peaceful. Sick, but peaceful.

I faced Dr. Gordon again. "What can we do?"

"I don't want to get your hopes up, but there is a clinical trial we can try…if we can get her enrolled in time, that is. It's a long shot." Her face softened in sympathy.

"Do it." I blinked away tears. "Do whatever you have to."

The doctor hesitated. "Getting her into the trial isn't the only issue. Like the last treatment, your insurance won't cover it. You've indicated your finances aren't—"

"I'll get the money. How soon can she get in?"

"I'll do my best, but you might want to prepare… making her comfortable is about all we can do at this point unless something changes."

I blinked several times until the sting in my eyes

abated. A knock sounded, and the door creaked open behind me. Dr. Gordon gave me one last sympathetic look. "I'll let the two of you visit."

I turned around in time to see her nod at Ian on her way out.

"Hi." His eyes traveled the length of my body, from the red locks of my hair to the spiky heels encasing my feet. "How was the business trip?"

"Exhausting." That much was true; Gage Channing had put me through the ringer. Nothing compared to this, though. My eyes burned with more unshed tears.

You are not breaking down in front of him.

I turned back to Eve and planted a kiss on her forehead. "Can you give me a minute?" I closed my eyes and breathed in her scent, and my throat tightened. "Please."

"What's wrong?" The rustling of his clothing reached my ears.

"The treatment isn't-isn't…"

"Kayla…I don't know what to say. " His breath whispered across the back of my neck. "I'm so sorry. I don't have any kids…I can't even begin to imagine what you're going through right now."

I couldn't stop despair from overflowing, and when I sensed him reaching for me, I jerked out of his grasp. "Please…don't." Speaking to him about my daughter was one thing, but allowing myself to fall apart in his embrace was another. I wouldn't be able to stop crying if he wrapped those strong arms around me; I remembered much too vividly the comfort and shelter they offered. I finally turned and faced him.

"Don't shut me out," he pleaded. "You need me…I'm here."

"Why now?" I was playing with fire, but I couldn't stop the question from escaping. "It's been seven years, Ian."

"Seven years too long." He shook his head. "You pushed me out of your life, moved away, wouldn't take my calls…why'd you disappear like that?"

"Can we not get into this right now?"

"We used to mean everything to each other." He drew in a breath. "I came back for you, Kayla."

I wanted to lean on him so badly. He'd been my rock, the one person I could trust no matter what. But leaning on him was off-limits. Gage would go ballistic if he found out I was talking to him. "Eve and I will be okay," I whispered, needing to believe it was true more than anything. "Dr. Gordon mentioned a clinical trial."

"She's a fighter," he said. "Just like her mom."

No three-year-old should have to fight so hard to live. Another piece of my heart broke off and shattered. If I lost Eve…I couldn't fathom living.

"Is there anything I can do?" he asked, looking about as helpless as I felt.

I shook my head. Ian couldn't step back into the role of protector and comforter…lover. Things change, and as much as I hated to admit it, the only person who could help me now was my sadistic boss. I'd do whatever Gage wanted, so long as he made sure my daughter had a fighting chance. With his money and resources…

"I just need some time. Please, Ian."

He ran his hand over his mouth and reluctantly nodded. "You know where to find me."

"I know."

He went to the door, and I sensed him wavering. "I've missed you," he said as he slipped from the room.

I stretched out next to Eve and pulled her into my arms. "I've missed you too."

12. SAFE NO MORE

It was fifteen past nine when I pounded on Gage's door.

He jerked it open, and I immediately recognized the hardened glint in his eyes. He halted and did a double take. I could only imagine what I must look like; tear-streaked face, drenched hair and clothes. I was broken on the inside and tattered on the outside. I imagined my eyes were depths of vacancy.

"I—" My voice hitched on a sob. Until that moment, I hadn't allowed myself to acknowledge how scared I was. I'd had so much hope that the treatment would work. Now it felt as if someone was gripping my heart and squeezing a little more as each second passed.

"What's wrong?"

"It's Eve…"

"Come here." He grabbed my arm and pulled me inside, and then he enfolded my shivering body into his arms. "What happened?"

I clung to him. "The treatment isn't working." A hiccup escaped as he rubbed some warmth back into my body. "I need more money. There's one last trial her doctor wants to try…" I untangled from his embrace and fell to my knees. "Please, Master. I'll do anything you want."

His hands sifted through my hair. "I'm a bastard for being so turned on right now. What I want is to hurt you. Will you let me?"

Nothing could hurt worse than the terror eating away at my insides. "Yes, Master. Do as you wish. Just save my daughter."

He pulled my hair until I tilted my head back. "Your lack of faith in me is insulting. I told you I'd take care of her."

"This is an additional cost, Master. A really expensive one."

"You have my assurance. I'll drop off another check at the hospital first thing in the morning." He paused, and his steady gaze froze me to the spot. "So long as you fully submit to me."

"Master…I have." I forced the words out. "I do."

He shook his head slowly, as if taking the time to weigh his words. "No, you haven't. Not completely. There's a strong, stubborn…*independent*…part of you that still resists."

I parted my lips, but nothing came out; what he said was true.

"Tonight won't be easy." His gaze lowered to my mouth. "I'm going to push you to your limits. I'm tired of playing games. I shouldn't have to punish you so often." He let go of my hair, and his face hardened with determination. "You want my help? I want your total submission. Are we clear?"

I searched his eyes for a spark of empathy and found the slightest hint of an ember. "Yes, Master."

"Did you break any of my rules?"

I chewed on my lip. "I made myself…" I really didn't want to say the words. My cheeks warmed at the memory because I'd been thinking of him as I came.

"Go on," he prompted.

"I made myself orgasm."

"How many times?"

"Once."

"Anything else?"

"I haven't eaten much today."

"I see." He frowned. "What is your least favorite food?"

I squinted up at him, wondering where he was going with this. "Master?"

"Answer the question."

"I guess…fish."

"Then you will eat fish every night this week for dinner. I'm sure this menu will make you grateful for the one I expect you to follow."

I became nauseated at the thought but wisely remained quiet. He'd proven time and again that arguing or questioning him wouldn't change the outcome of what he decided, and I couldn't afford to piss him off. I needed to be on my best behavior…

Do it for Eve.

"As for your forbidden orgasm, you'll be denied again

tonight. Get up."

My stomach dropped as I stood. Wordlessly, he led me down to the basement. Rather than turn on the lights, Gage took the time to set several candles ablaze. "Strip."

I obeyed his command without hesitation. Our eyes never wavered as I shed my clothing piece by piece. My nipples ached, forming two hard pebbles that drew his hungry gaze, and the magic spot between my legs began to throb. I swallowed the self-loathing that rose in my throat.

"Leave the heels on. I like them." He held out a hand. "Come."

I slid my hand into his, and in that moment—a moment I instinctively recognized as a pivotal one—I knew I'd succumbed. I was at his mercy, and there was no going back. The fear still lingered, as did hatred, but renewed purpose filled me. The confusing part was how I hated and craved him so much at the same time.

Gage led me over to the big X on the wall. I couldn't stop shivering as he encircled my wrists and ankles with chains.

"I'm so cold, Master."

"You won't be for long." He pushed me against the wall, and his dexterous fingers locked me in place. I stood spread-eagled, naked except for my heels.

"I want to void your safe word, but I'll leave the choice up to you."

Why did this feel like a trick? "Why, Master?"

"It'll be a sign that you've given yourself to me completely. You said you'd do anything, and I believe you.

Will you relinquish your safe word?"

I swallowed hard. "For tonight?"

"No, until our contract ends."

A shiver drifted across my breasts. He wanted to shatter my last thread of resistance. There would be nothing to stop him from doing as he wished—not that there was much now that would cease his torture. But knowing I'd had the option to end it at any time… somehow that small, inconsequential thing made his demands bearable. Now, if I couldn't handle what he dished out, my only option would be to flee and turn myself in.

"I-I can't use it, Master. I can't go to jail."

"It's a yes or no question, Kayla."

I wanted to say no. Something deep inside—self-preservation, perhaps—set the word on the tip of my tongue. Yet…if I eliminated the option, there would be no way out. I'd never have to face the temptation of wagering Eve's life against my pain and torture. She'd be safer this way.

"Yes."

"Are you sure?"

"Yes, Master."

He moved quickly, taking my sight with a blindfold, the ability to beg and plead with a ball gag. Nausea rose with panic, and my heartbeat thundered in my ears as he silenced everything with earplugs. I could hear nothing past the roar in my head, see nothing beyond the suffocating darkness pressing on me. Gage had effectively isolated me within my own mind. I made protesting, terrified pleas—garbled muffles to my plugged ears—and pulled against the restraints. Legs trembling violently, I barely had the strength to keep myself upright. Had I not been chained to the wall, I would have crumbled to the floor.

What have I done?

At the first graze of his teeth to my nipple, every muscle in my body stiffened. I held my breath, not knowing if he planned to serve pain or pleasure, and not knowing was excruciating. He sucked my nipple into the scorching cavity of his mouth. I wasn't sure if I whimpered or moaned—maybe it was a little of both. His fingers teased my other breast, and he trailed a hand down my stomach, making my muscles quiver beneath his touch. He dipped a finger into my wetness, teasing a moment before he pulled away.

Nothing could have prepared me for the first strike between my thighs. I would have screamed if he'd left me with the choice. Good God, he was whipping my most intimate place. He wasn't kidding when he said he wanted to hurt me. My legs cramped with each strike, and I sobbed for mercy as tears escaped the blindfold.

Several long minutes passed. I was beginning to grow numb when the heat of his mouth replaced the whip. I jerked to my toes as his tongue swirled the pain away with expert strokes, delving deeper as he simultaneously released my ankles from the restraints. He lifted me, urged my legs around his shoulders, and probed my ass with a finger as he kissed me intimately. The closer his tongue brought me to oblivion, the more I gave myself over to him.

I wanted to come so badly—was certain I begged for it in muffled pleas—but knew it was off-limits. Gage Channing knew how to take a woman to the edge, and he was even better at pulling back at the last second. He did it relentlessly. Tears dripped from my chin onto my heaving breasts, and I could think of nothing but how I wish he'd let me come…let me fall into oblivion where nothing had the power to touch me.

He abruptly pulled away, leaving me suspended in a combination of anticipation and apprehension. I had no way to measure time, and the longer he left me there— bound, gagged, unable to see, hear, or speak—the closer I reached hysteria. Where was he? Surely he wouldn't leave me alone like this? In the midst of my thundering heartbeat, I suddenly remembered his words over the weekend.

"You need to learn to trust me."

Was this a test? Gage wasn't careless—he'd said as much himself. He was probably standing in front of me, enjoying my internal struggle not to let blinding panic take over. I couldn't help but wonder what made a man like him tick. He'd certainly pushed me to my limits and beyond, and I was positive he was sporting a raging erection at witnessing my helplessness.

I jerked when something cold pressed against my nipples, and when he clamped them to an unbearable pinch, I screeched around the gag, my throat on fire from the strain. Only his tongue on my clit had the power to distract me. He took me to the edge again, almost pushed me over, but like the cruel sadist he was, he pulled away at the last second. Gage removed the gag, blindfold, earplugs…released my hands. I slumped into his arms, and his mouth plundered mine as he carried me to bed. We dipped into the mattress as one.

"Do you belong to me?" Bracing above me, he looked into my eyes.

"Yes, Master," I mumbled, studying him through the haze. "Why do you like to hurt me?"

He brushed a lock of hair out of my eyes. Several moments went by, in which he ran his hands through my hair, trailed his fingers down my collarbone, and teased the valley between my breasts. He pulled on the clamps and yanked painfully.

"Knowing that I can do anything to you, that I can bring you intense pain or pleasure…there's no better feeling than that."

His mouth was on mine before I was able to respond. He removed the clamps and fondled my breasts, then squeezed and pinched, refusing to let go until I begged him to stop. Sitting back long enough to unbutton his slacks, he kicked them off before carelessly flinging them across the room. He attacked my mouth again, burying his hands in my hair as he wedged apart my legs. I moaned deep in my throat as he slid into me.

This was not the Gage I'd come to know over the weekend. This man was different, his brutality in direct contrast with his gentleness; he confused the heck out of me. So did my eager response to him. He laced our fingers together and held my hands to the bed. Every thrust was sensual yet demanding, each plunge a testament of his possession and power.

"Look at me, Kayla."

I found his eyes and couldn't have looked away if I tried.

"Who am I?"

"My Master…" I curled my fingers around his until my nails bit into his skin. He didn't even flinch. I arched up to meet his thrusts. "I want you," I gasped. "Let me come, Master."

"No." He let go of my hands and gripped my hair, yanking my head back hard. "Control it, you don't have my permission. I'll deny you all weekend if you disobey me."

"Oh God! Please…I can't…please…"

He pulled out and pumped his cock in the palm of his hand until he spilled onto my stomach.

I stared at him in shock. I'd been so out of my mind, I'd failed to notice that he hadn't used a condom. The mixture of our heavy breathing filled the basement for several long moments. Gage broke it with a voice left husky from his orgasm.

"I want nothing more than to make you come. When I do, you'll never want to leave me." He collapsed beside me and rolled onto his back.

I shuddered at the implication of his words. For the first time since entering into this madness, I doubted his intentions. What if he wanted more from me than six weeks? What the hell was I supposed to do then?

"Your daughter is going to be okay." The change of

subject intruded upon my thoughts, and a different fear arose.

"I don't know what I'll do if she…"

"I'll do everything in my power to make sure she has the best doctors, the best treatments."

I rolled to my side and looked at him. "Thank you."

He grabbed my chin. "Who am I?" His eyes hypnotized me as they searched my face.

"You're my Master."

"I'll hold up my end of the bargain, so long as you hold up yours." He gave me a wry smile. "I'm not heartless, Kayla, despite what you might think when I'm whipping you or shoving my cock into this tempting mouth of yours." He cradled my head and kissed me; a deep, tender exchange of tongues that made me throb between my legs all over again. He broke away and brushed his thumb across my lips. "I can't wait to fuck you here again."

My heart thudded at the reminder. "What about the gossip at work, Master? Someone found out."

"I'll take care of it. I have an idea of who's behind the rumors. She's only guessing because she's been in my office on her knees a time or two."

I wanted to ask if it was Katherine but refrained from giving voice to the question. "How do you know, Master?"

"Nothing goes on in my office without my knowing."

Gage sat up and pulled on his slacks. "I'll have a new contract drawn up to eliminate your safe word." He paused for a moment. "This changes things, Kayla. It's more responsibility for both of us. I'm giving you a homework assignment to help you prepare for what's to come. I want you to write a thousand word research paper on what it means to be a slave. I expect you to learn how to please and obey me."

Dread sat heavy in my gut, and I wondered what I'd gotten myself into.

"And I have one more stipulation, non-negotiable." He got to his feet and turned to me. "I demand absolute honesty from you. No lies, and no withholding anything from me. If I find out you've lied or kept something from me, you won't be punished—you'll go straight to jail. Do you understand?"

A lump formed in my throat, and I swallowed. "There's something you need to know, Master."

"What is it?"

"The man from college…the one you asked about? He's back. He works at the hospital."

"Why is this something you think I need to know?"

"Because he's stopped by Eve's room a couple of times, Master."

Gage's mouth flattened into a hard line. "Then you'll tell him you don't want to see him again." He zipped up his pants and gave me a hard look. "And you won't. I'll see you tomorrow at the office. Don't forget to write in your journal tonight, and for God's sakes, go eat something. You're already so damn thin."

He climbed the stairs without a backward glance.

13. OFFICE POLITICS

I didn't know what to expect the following morning when I arrived at work, but I had to admit to being shocked that not a single person looked my way as I exited the elevator. Most noticeable was Katherine's absence. An older woman sat in her place; she answered the phone as I passed by on my way to Gage's office. Holding his coffee in one hand, I knocked on his door with the other…and froze as a loud moan filtered through. I was debating on what to do when the door jerked open a few moments later. Katherine aimed her iciest glare in my direction as she brushed by me.

"Come in, Kayla." Gage casually zipped his pants and took a seat behind his desk. "Shut the door."

I went to do as told, only I didn't merely shut the damn thing—I slammed my fingers in the process. "Ow!" The coffee dropped to my feet, coating my heels in brown liquid. Gage shot up and crossed the office before I could take a breath.

"Let me see." He grabbed my hand and inspected my

fingers. "They're a little purple, but they don't appear broken."

I couldn't see beyond the front of his pants; he hadn't tucked in his shirt fully. "Did I do something wrong, Master?"

His eyes zeroed in on my face, eyebrows slightly raised. "Why would you think that?"

"Well…I'm assuming Katherine was in here doing what I…did yesterday?"

His mouth twitched. "Does that bother you?"

Not for the reason he apparently assumed it did. I couldn't afford to displease him, and if he felt the need to go to other women… "No, I just don't want to displease you, Master." I'd started my research the previous night and had been overwhelmed with information. Being a "proper" or "good" slave wouldn't be the easiest thing I ever did. I was beginning to understand what Gage wanted from me; he wanted me meek and pliable, willing to drop to my knees on demand and obey his every command. He expected me to anticipate his needs, as his pleasure was to be my first priority, as was serving him.

The center of my being revolted at the notion, but I'd do it for Eve.

"You do please me."

"Do you want me on my knees, Master?"

"No. We'll keep our office relationship as normal as possible, notwithstanding special circumstances." He tilted my chin up so I met his gaze head on. "Katherine was in here because I fired her. Considering what she pulled yesterday, sucking my cock was a fitting punishment." He smirked. "Or rather, my reaction afterward was. She thought she could manipulate me with her mouth."

Hadn't I had a similar thought yesterday? What the hell was happening to me? He was drawing me in, and I was helpless to stop it. Just remembering how he had the power to cast me into a void so intense in pleasure was enough to stall my breath. I was addicted to that void... that blissful escape from reality. I'd stumbled onto the term "subspace," and now I wondered if Gage was sending me there with every strike of his whip, every scorching touch of his mouth and hands. I couldn't deny he was one of the sexiest men I'd set eyes on, and on some level I was very much attracted to him, whether I liked it or not.

But I wasn't in love with him. I'd move on when our six weeks ended.

"What are you thinking?" he asked.

"Am I that obvious?"

"You wear everything on your face, Kayla. You always have."

My first instinct was to lie, but then I remembered his non-negotiable terms—terms I assumed he'd have me sign today. "I was thinking how I'd move on from you when this is all over."

His eyes darkened. "Can't wait to get away from me, huh?"

I wrung my hands. "You won't like the truth, Master."

"Maybe not, but I demand it."

"I can't be who you want me to be. I'll pretend for

Eve's sake, and I'll do whatever I have to in the meantime, but it'll be a lie. As soon as our six weeks are up, I'll walk."

Gage slid his hand along my cheek. "We'll see." He returned to his desk. "The company Christmas party is this Friday night. We'll attend together." He'd switched gears so fast, my head spun.

"Won't that fuel the gossip?"

He waved away my concern. "No one will dare treat you badly after today. You have nothing to worry about." He leaned back in his chair. "As far as anyone needs to know, you and I are dating. I'm not about to squander the opportunity to have you on my arm for the next five weeks." He focused his attention on his computer. "Let's get to work."

I hastily pulled out my iPad as he began dictating to me. After he'd armed me with the day's instructions, he slid a piece of paper across the desk. "Your new contract. No safe word, and no lies." A pen accompanied the paper.

My hand shook as I scrawled my name at the bottom. "Master...will you let me visit Eve on Friday? I won't be long—I just can't stand the thought of going a whole two days without seeing her, especially now that her condition is so rocky."

"I'll give you an hour. And if you behave well, you can call the hospital on Saturday too."

"Thank you." I let out a breath. Deep down, I hadn't expected him to say yes.

"Speaking of the hospital, do you expect to get a visit

from Dr. Kaplan this evening?"

I froze at his words. "I don't know, Master."

"Don't forget what you have to do. I want him out of your life, is that clear?"

"Yes, Master."

"Good, then I'll see you at lunchtime." Gage casually dismissed me as he went back to work.

I left his office, and only after I'd closed the door did it occur to me that I'd never mentioned Ian's name.

14. REMINISCENT RAIN

The week passed amidst a torrential downpour before I saw Ian again. Caught up in the daily grind of work and spending every free moment at the hospital, I wasn't prepared to face him yet. If I was being honest, I wouldn't ever be ready to cast him aside again. I watched Eve slumber peacefully, grateful for the hour Gage had given me, and thought back to the day seven years ago when I told Ian goodbye. We'd stood in my driveway, too consumed with despair to care about the rainstorm soaking us. After being inseparable friends for three years, we'd finally given in to the feelings neither of us could deny any longer. If I had to list my favorite moments in life, that night with Ian would be at the top. No one had ever made me feel the way he had…cherished, worshipped, loved.

But then everything fell apart when I realized I was pregnant with Rick's baby. Rick and I had been together for a year—a rocky on-again, off-again year filled with screaming arguments and too many tears to count. He'd revealed a hint of his dark nature as the months went by: jealous, possessive, mean-spirited. I'd eventually hit a crossroads—either continue down a destructive path with him, or risk my friendship with Ian by turning it into something more. I'd chosen the latter, experienced a small taste of happiness, and had thrown it all away before something truly amazing could bloom. Going back to my ex had been a misguided attempt at doing the right thing by my baby.

How naive I'd been. I closed my eyes to the memory of that first beating, the one that began them all…the one that ended my first pregnancy just shy of twelve weeks. Even now I asked myself why I'd stayed so long… even knowing how I would never regret the decision; Eve wouldn't be here if I'd left sooner. I didn't allow myself to think of the past often, but I didn't have a choice now. The memories seeped through the cracks of the metaphorical room in which I'd locked them. They flooded me, especially the night I'd told Ian I didn't love him. Raindrops had disguised his tears, but not the devastation in the depths of those hazel eyes I still dreamed about seven years later.

"Hey, if you're gonna cry every time I come near you, maybe I should bring chocolate." I raised my head and found the object of my thoughts standing in the doorway. He frowned, despite the light tone of his words, and closed the door behind him. "How's Eve?"

I took a deep breath. "You should go."

"You have a habit of telling me that." He folded his arms and leaned against the door.

"I can't handle seeing you right now. Eve started a new treatment yesterday, and I'm under a lot of pressure at work right now…" *Under Gage Channing's watchful eye.* "I'm glad you're back, but I think we need a few weeks to let things settle first."

"Meaning you're gonna barricade yourself from people and deal with her illness alone." He shook his head and pulled up a chair, legs scraping the linoleum, and settled across from me on the other side of the bed. "You look like hell. Have you gotten any sleep at all?"

"Not much," I admitted quietly. Unable to tear myself away as the weekend approached, I'd slept at Eve's bedside for the past two nights. "You really need to go."

He leaned forward, and his eyes—greener today than usual—froze me to the spot. "Don't shut me out. I won't walk away this time. I've regretted it every day for seven years."

"I need you to stay away from me and Eve for the next few weeks. Please…I'm begging you."

"Why?"

"I can't tell you—" I broke off, cringing at the slip-up. "Please, just go."

"You're worrying me, Kayla." He rubbed a hand down his face and sighed. "What's going on with you?"

"Nothing." Firming my resolve, I met his unyielding stare. "I need for you to leave me alone. I don't want to see you, or hear from you—"

He sprung to his feet, and every muscle in his body tensed. "So we're doing this again? Is it someone else? If you're involved with someone, just say so. I won't like it, but I can deal with it." He shoved his hands into his pockets, and his shoulders relaxed a fraction as he waited for a reply.

Waited for me to deny it.

I stared at my shoes—spiky heels that made my feet ache and reminded me of the man who'd trapped me. Saying I was seeing someone would be the easiest solution to this dilemma. "There's no one else." I looked up and met Ian's gaze. "There's no one else," I repeated. "I just need time."

"Take all the time you need." He flung the door open. "I hope you don't take another seven years to figure it out."

15. LIE DETECTOR

I stood on Gage's doorstep, allowing myself one last minute of reflection before I entered his domain of pain. Ian's stormy exit from my life—once again—still clung to my emotions, making me susceptible to acts of unpredictability. I couldn't afford feeling this way when Gage opened that door. The foundation of my acquiescence had shifted since I'd first stood in this spot a week ago...funny, how it seemed much longer. I no longer had a safe word, but more importantly, I owed Gage. Whatever he'd done, whatever strings he'd pulled, had gotten Eve into the trial faster than her doctor thought possible. I couldn't mess this up. Forcing my turbulent thoughts to the back of my mind, I knocked on his door.

He treated me to a real smile from the other side. "Right on time. I take it you've learned your lesson this week?" He raised an eyebrow.

"Yes, Master," I said as he ushered me into the foyer.

He held out his hand. "Your journal?"

I removed it from my oversized purse. "The research paper is tucked in the back."

"Go ahead and put your things in the closet," he instructed as he flipped through the pages. "Did you break anymore rules?"

"No, Master."

He smiled in a way that made my stomach drop. The smile of the devil. "For your sake, I hope you're telling the truth. Lie detectors aren't easy to fool."

"What are you talking about, Master?"

"You'll undergo a polygraph." Setting the journal aside, he grabbed my arm and led me into a home office. A wall of windows opened to a view of the swimming pool in the backyard. If not for the nervous flutters in my stomach, I would have laughed; only Gage Channing would have an outdoor pool in the Pacific Northwest. Rain beat against the glass, and watching all that water made me shiver.

We weren't alone. Someone sat behind the desk where an odd machine was displayed on the surface. "Have a seat," he invited with a reassuring smile.

"This is Mr. Hughes," Gage said as I slid into a chair. "He's aware of the nature of our relationship, so there's no need to feel uncomfortable at the intimacy of the questions. He's heard it all, trust me."

I quirked an eyebrow but didn't voice my incredulity.

"I'll be back when you've finished." Gage pinned me to the chair with his deep blue eyes. "I'll advise you not to lie here, Kayla."

I hadn't planned to, but that still didn't calm my

apprehension. Lie detectors weren't fail-proof, were they?

"Don't be nervous," Mr. Hughes said after Gage had disappeared through the doorway. "Just be honest and everything will go smoothly."

Sure, says the guy administering the test. I folded my hands in my lap and remained silent as he hooked me up to the machine. He pressed a few buttons, made some adjustments, and pulled out a sheet of paper.

"Do you take any medications?"

"No."

He asked several more questions—all of them related to my personal and medical background. "All right, I'm going to ask you two questions that you'll answer yes to. This is to calibrate the machine." He cleared his throat. "Is your name Kayla Sutton?"

"Yes."

"Do you live in Europe?"

"Yes."

He cleared his throat again and peered at the paper in his hands. "Let's begin. Did you have any inappropriate contact with a man other than your Master?"

I swallowed hard and thought about Ian. Considering he hadn't even touched me, and I'd only spoken to him briefly to push him out of my life—probably for good—I was fairly certain in my answer. "No."

"Did you break any of your Master's rules?"

"N-no."

Mr. Hughes marked something on the printout. "Did you eat fish for dinner every night this week?"

"Yes."

"Did you take off your Master's collar?"

"No."

"Did you masturbate?"

My face burned at such an intimate question. "No." But God, how I'd wanted to.

He asked a few more questions, and when it was over I experienced the sweetest sense of relief. Gage reentered the room after I'd been unhooked from the machine.

"Did she pass?"

"Yes."

"Go on down to the basement and prepare. I'll be down shortly."

"Yes, Master." I hurried from the room and entered the basement with flaming cheeks. That had been more mortifying than going to the gynecologist. A few moments snuck by as I leaned against the door, breathing heavy as uncertainty took hold of me. He wanted me to "prepare." I suddenly felt lost; without Gage to dictate my every move, I wasn't sure what to do. Descending the stairs, I entered his "dungeon" and remembered how the cold leather of the bench chilled my skin, how the sharp sting of his whip struck with the speed of a snake; and more recently how that strip of leather had the power to set my crotch on fire…how his tongue ignited a different kind of burn.

I stepped into the room, brought my fingers to my blouse, and began unhooking the buttons. Instinctively, I knew what he wanted. My nipples pebbled in the chilly air, and as I laid my clothing neatly on the couch, tingles shivered to my toes. I moved to the center of the floor and fell to my knees.

And closed my eyes and waited.

A drift of air was the only indication he'd entered. His clothes whispered as he came near, and I hated myself for craving the warmth he radiated.

Dampness flooded the spot between my thighs. I craved much more than body heat. Gage had done something to me—flipped a switch—and despite the harsh punishments he issued, I yearned for another taste of explosive liberation. I'd taken it once without permission; somehow, I knew he'd send me into another realm when he coaxed an orgasm from me of his own free will. It was that foggy-headed reality I hungered for most—a time when thought wasn't possible, when pain and difficult decisions didn't exist. Gage had enslaved me, and by doing so he also freed me on some level.

"Are you ready to fully submit, Kayla?"

"Yes, Master."

He ran a hand over my hair. "Why are you on your knees?"

"To please you, Master."

He groaned. "You are, baby, and I can't wait to return the favor." My heart began to race. The haze was taking over already, and he had barely touched me. "Though your pleasure will come with pain." He tilted my chin up. "Did you send the doctor away?"

"Yes, Master."

"How did he take it?"

Ian's angry, hurt expression flashed in my mind. "Not well."

"And he won't come back?"

I blinked. "I don't think so."

"How does that make you feel?"

"Upset, Master." The truth spilled from my lips without thought or effort. The way he commanded my compliance, his strong voice floating above me as I knelt on the hard floor, reinforced the dynamics of our relationship.

"Yet you obeyed me, and you're being truthful about it."

"Yes, Master. I told you I was yours, and I meant it." Five more weeks. I could give him that.

"I needed to know you'd be honest with me no matter what. Your absolute honesty is important to me. I'll accept nothing less."

"I know, Master." It was one of two rules I would never break, the other being confidentiality.

He slipped a blindfold over my eyes before guiding me to my feet. "Undress me," he said, bringing my hands to his shirt.

I fumbled with the buttons, blindly undoing them. His shirt whispered to the floor, and my hands drifted to his belt. Sliding it from the loops reminded me of the beating I'd taken in his office earlier that week. I shuddered at the thought and reached for what I thought was the button of his slacks. Instead I found his erection straining against the zipper. He jerked my hands up a few inches and helped me remove the last barrier to his body.

"Good girl." He pressed down on my shoulders until I sank to my knees again. Unlike in his office, where he'd given me most of the control, he swatted my hands away, grabbed my head, and forced his cock between my lips. I gagged the deeper he dove, but that didn't deter him. I couldn't see his expression, but I imagined the tightness of his features, the tension in his shoulders as he neared climax. I didn't fight him as he slipped in and out, his balls flapping against my chin. The loud groan he released as he spilled into my mouth sent fire between my legs. I ached in a way that was exhilarating and humiliating all at once—the two emotions fought for space in my heart. No matter how many times he forced me to my knees, demanded I bend to his will, my body still responded in a primal way even I didn't understand.

Gage expelled a heavy breath. "You know how to love a man's cock."

I raised my head and waited for his instruction.

He removed the blindfold. "We have a Christmas party to get to." Gage helped me to my feet, and I gasped when he spun me around and pushed me to the bed. "Bend over." I hadn't noticed the cocktail dress he'd set out on the mattress…or the butt plug and nipples clamps. I cringed to think of the pain those things would inflict.

"You'll wear them to the party," he said, as if he'd heard my thoughts. He grabbed the plug, and I tensed in preparation, hissing a breath through my teeth as he pushed it in. He grabbed my arm and twirled me until I faced him again. I shrank away when he reached for the clamps.

"I-I'm sorr—"

"Don't be sorry, Kayla. Just obey. I can restrain you,

if you won't behave yourself."

I shook my head and stepped toward him.

His eyes lingered on my nipples, and the edges of his mouth turned up. "Stand up straight and clasp your hands behind your back. You'll learn to present your breasts properly."

I lengthened my spine and laced my fingers together at the small of my back, and the position put my chest on display. He bent down and slid his tongue across each nipple. A delicious chill raced through me, only to be obliterated when he clamped the first sensitive peak. I whimpered, and Gage responded by tightening the clamp further. I screwed my eyes shut as he did the same to the other side. I could only imagine how excruciating they'd feel if I hadn't breastfed.

He brought his mouth to my ear. "I want you uncomfortable. I want your tits aching, your ass full. By the time we return tonight, you'll beg me to fill every part of you."

A shiver of excitement tore through me.

"Get dressed. Come upstairs when you're ready." His lips drifted down my chest, and he bit down on the chain connecting my breasts and pulled. "Don't take too long—we're almost late."

I dressed quickly, gritting my teeth as the material scraped across my aching nipples, and then climbed the stairs. Gage's voice rang through the house as I edged the door open, though judging by his low tone, I figured he didn't want to be overheard. Whoever was on the other end of the call had sure pushed a button.

"I'm tired of your threats!" he hissed.

I should have announced my presence, but in the end my curious nature won. I pressed against the door and listened.

"You have no idea who you're dealing with, do you?" Silence followed, until he muttered something indistinguishable. The sound of his feet hitting the floor reverberated in my ears. I scrambled to open the door behind me, and when Gage rounded the corner, it appeared as if I'd just exited. He smoothed the anger from his features and ended the call. "Ready to go?"

"Yeah…" My mouth parted, and I couldn't help but stare at the sight of Gage Channing in a tux.

16. CHAMPAGNE AND LUST

The Sheraton Hotel hosted the company Christmas party. Gage opened the door for me and then tucked my arm in his as we approached the room where the event was being held. Everyone in the room took notice upon our arrival, but Gage was correct in people's reactions. Apparently, Katherine's absence served as a reminder for people to mind their own business.

Gage nuzzled my neck and spoke into my ear. "Would you like some champagne?"

I nodded, unable to speak.

He leaned into me. "Enjoy yourself tonight. You'll have plenty of time to surrender to me later." My breath went thready at his words. Gage planted a kiss on my cheek before heading in the direction of the bar.

The instant I was alone, Jody waltzed up to me. I'd known her for years, and it was on her referral that I'd gotten the job. I frowned when I realized we'd barely spoken, let alone spent time together, since she'd moved on from Channing Enterprises. She'd left months ago, around the time I'd been promoted to Gage's personal assistant, to take a job as managing accountant at a smaller firm.

"Are you really dating Gage?"

My cheeks warmed. "Is that what everyone's saying?"

She nodded. "Holy smokes, Kayla, the man is hot." She raised her eyebrows and shot me a playful grin. "I should know—like most of the female employees at Channing Enterprises, I've had a turn at him."

"Are you serious?" I leaned closer and lowered my voice. "When?"

"A few years ago. Around the time you and Rick split."

"I hadn't realized you'd worked for him that long."

"Yep. I still miss it sometimes." She gazed across the room at her date, who I vaguely recognized from the mail room. "That's why I finagled a plus one from Rob. I couldn't pass up this party." She winked at me. "Good to see you again. We should do lunch sometime."

"I'd like that."

"Great," she said as Rob gestured at her. "Oops, gotta go. Rob's a hot one too, though he's not into kink like Gage was. Is he still into that shit?" she threw the question over her shoulder.

The butt plug vibrated to life for a moment, and I gulped. Is that what they were calling it? Kink?

Gage returned a few moments later, champagne in hand. Sporting a knowing smirk, he handed me a crystal flute. "Dinner's about to start." He ushered me to a table. The room was decorated in whites, blacks, and silvers, with splashes of red and gold. The tables were adorned with black table cloths and silver candles. White linens accompanied the red and gold patterned china. A huge Christmas tree took up one corner of the room. Gage pulled out a chair and gestured for me to take a seat. He settled next to me and immediately placed his hand on my knee.

Two other couples joined us, and conversation revolved around work for the short period before dinner was served. As the meal wore on, Gage inched his hand up my thigh. Certain my cheeks were turning the color of tomato paste, I leaned away from him, but all that got me was a hard look and more determination on his part. He carried on his conversation easily as he forced my thighs apart.

My only defense was to focus on cutting my chicken into small bites and chewing until the meat practically slid down my throat. I bit my tongue when his fingers slipped inside my panties. His touch scorched me from the inside out, and suddenly, the heavy ache in my nipples only added fuel to his public seduction. God…armed with sexual frustration and champagne, I became dizzy with it and prayed no one would guess what was going on underneath the table. He tilted his head and gave me a knowing smile as he stroked me, spreading my wetness to my clit. His other hand disappeared under the table, and the plug vibrated to life in my ass again. I gripped my chair and took a deep breath through my nose.

"So, Kayla, how is Eve?"

What a way to douse the fire. I cast my attention on

the woman across from me, and though I couldn't remember her name, I was more than grateful for the distraction. "It's been up and down, but her doctor is confident this new trial will help."

Gage slid a finger inside, and a groan escaped.

The woman furrowed her brows. "Are you all right? You don't look well, dear."

I sprang up from the table. "I think it was something I ate. Please, excuse me." I nearly crashed into the women's restroom in my haste to escape Gage. A quick check of the stalls assured me I was alone. Grabbing hold of the counter, I focused on breathing and closed my eyes, but the plug still vibrated incessantly, making me moan as my insides clenched.

The door creaked open, and Gage entered. "Are you alone in here?"

I nodded.

He locked the door, and I watched his reflection wearily, wondering if I'd earned myself another punishment for bolting from the table. He stood behind me and rested his hands next to mine, caging me in between the counter and his impressive body. Pure desire reflected from his eyes in the mirror—a maniacal glint that both frightened and excited me. We said nothing as we stared at each other, and when Gage removed his hands, I didn't dare move. He gripped my skirt and inched it up before sliding his hand beneath my panties again.

"Your eyes darken to the deepest brown when you're turned on, did you realize that?"

"No," I said on a moan. My head fell back against his shoulder, and his lips devoured my throat as he stroked me.

"You're so wet, baby."

I groaned and arched into his hand. "What are you doing to me?"

"Making you mine." He took my mouth, and I kissed him back with abandon, chasing his tongue again and again.

"I'm losing myself to you," I gasped, tearing my mouth from his.

"Not yet, you're not." He stepped away. "Come back to the table."

Five minutes later I obeyed, only stumbling twice on my journey back to my seat. Dessert had already been served. Gage wasted no time in reclaiming the hot, damp place between my legs. He stroked me relentlessly, and not even the decadent cake had the power to distract me. By the time he pulled me into his arms on the dance floor, I'd downed four more glasses of champagne and was more than a little tipsy. Bodies flush, our champagne breaths mingling, I melted against him and let him pull me into the sway. Something shifted within me during that dance. For the first time, I returned his touch. Sliding my hands into his hair, I curled my fingers into the dark strands as he swept me across the room. I didn't care if everyone was watching, if what I was doing and feeling was wrong.

And it was so wrong. Nothing about this situation should feel romanticized, but I was lost and never wanted to be found.

He tightened his arms around me, pulling me close enough that his hard-on strained against my stomach. "Wanna get out of here?"

Our faces were inches apart, and for a moment I thought he was going to kiss me in front of everyone. "Yeah."

We left in a flurry of goodbyes, and the only thing more dizzying than my champagne-induced state was the commotion of grabbing our coats. The drive back to Gage's place was but a fuzzy memory. We stumbled through the front door, his mouth hot and wet on my throat as my thighs locked around his waist. My hands gripped his hair as he carried me through the house. Maybe later I'd question why he took me to his bedroom instead of the basement, or why he seemed so un-Gage like as he ripped the bodice of my dress in an impatient fit of desire. The material tore to my waist, exposing my clamped breasts. He yanked on the chain, propelling me toward him and the bed, and his mouth closed over an aching nipple. We shed our clothing and tumbled onto the mattress, where he wrapped my fingers around the bars of the headboard.

"Don't let go." His breath fanned across my face an instant before he blinded me with a silk tie. "I'm going to remove the clamps." My heart jackhammered under his touch, and I squeezed the bars as blood rushed to my nipples, flooding them with pain.

His mouth moved over my breasts. "Tell me what you want," he whispered.

"I want you."

"Be specific, Kayla."

I bent my knees and spread wide for him. "I want you inside of me."

He pulled away, and though I couldn't see him, I imagined him gazing down at me, eyes the color of sapphires as he savored my surrender. He splayed his hands on my inner thighs, spreading me further and torturing me with the tickle of his thumbs. "Tell me more."

"I-I want…you sliding in and out slowly, your mouth on my breasts…everywhere." I sucked in a breath when he reached around and lifted me. "I want to feel you everywhere, Master."

He scooted down and smothered his face against my mound. I bucked against his mouth as his kiss spread through my body—in the tingle along my spine, in the ache of my curling feet. My fingers tightened a death grip around the bars, and I dug my feet into the mattress, meeting each thrust of his tongue and fingers.

He slid up my stomach and plunged into me without warning, filling me so fully, I almost climaxed.

"You feel so fucking good." He buried his face in my hair and folded his hands around mine, and we began to move, building a tempo that was both tender and explosive—a contradiction comparable to Gage. "Don't come until I give you permission."

I gritted my teeth as he moved inside me. It wasn't going to take much to send me over the edge, but knowing Gage, he'd probably do this all night before he let me come. Our bodies slicked together like two lovers on the beach oiled down with coconut lotion. Muscles tensing, moans escalating, we chased release. I wrenched my hands from underneath his and gripped his shoulders.

"I can't hold back much longer. Master…please…"

He removed the blindfold and froze, going perfectly still. The light from the hall illuminated the apprehension in his features. "Do you hate me?"

I blinked. "What?"

"You heard me. Do you hate me for what I've done to you?"

I parted my lips, denial on the tip of my tongue, but denying it would be dishonest. "Part of me does, Master." I closed my eyes on a sigh and raised my hips. "The other part can't get enough."

He groaned and sunk his hands into my hair. I was about to burst when he reared up onto his knees and carried me with him.

Clinging to him, I panted. "Please…"

"Say you'll never leave me."

"I'll never leave you." The lie escaped before I could stop it. I'd sunk so far into the abyss, I didn't know which way was up anymore.

"Come for me now, baby," he commanded, burrowing even deeper.

"Gage!" I screamed as the orgasm tore through me. I wrapped my body around his and rode the waves, digging my fingernails into his shoulders so hard, I was sure I drew blood.

17. RETREAT

Gage awoke me the next morning with breakfast in bed. As soon as I sat up, I gripped my throbbing head.

"Hungover?" he asked, setting the tray on the nightstand. He held out two white tablets and a glass of orange juice.

I nodded, and then swished down the pills.

"I'm afraid we hit the champagne a little too heavily last night. Now we'll both have to suffer the consequences." He sat down next to me, and only then did I notice the belt in his hand. My eyes shot to his. He immediately adverted his gaze. "Last night was… incredible…but that doesn't give you free rein to call me anything other than Master."

"I-I'm sorry, Master. It just slipped out." His name had more than slipped out; I'd screamed it to high heaven as I came undone in his arms.

He rose to his feet. "I am too, Kayla. Let's get this over with." He gestured to the space in front of him. "On your feet. Bend over and grab your ankles."

I slid from bed, and as I held onto my ankles, preparing for the strike of his belt, I went back to despising myself. He'd gotten to me last night, had snuck into a small corner of my heart. Now that little piece shattered to dust.

Bastard.

I mentally chanted the epithet with every strike, though I had to admit the punishment hurt more on an emotional level than a physical one; perhaps I'd gotten under his skin as well because he was now going easy on me, though recognizing that didn't make me feel any better.

Gage calmly put his belt away once he was satisfied I'd been thoroughly punished. "I promised you a phone call. Check on your daughter." He handed me his cell phone.

I studied him, trying to find a hint of the man I'd seen last night hiding under his cool exterior, but all I found was impenetrable steel. "Why do you do this?"

He tilted his head. "Do what?"

"Shut yourself off from emotion."

His body stiffened. "Are you *trying* to earn another punishment?"

I stepped closer and placed my hand on his chest; he flinched under my touch. "I'm trying to understand you." I peeked up and met his eyes. "You're tender one minute, and a brute the next. I can't keep up with your mood swings."

"You know nothing about me, except that disobeying will earn you another punishment." He gestured toward the bed. "Bend over the bed this time."

I turned and placed my hands on the mattress. "I know you care enough to let me contact Eve." The snap of his belt made me jump. I couldn't hold back a yelp as it landed on my bottom.

"Stop analyzing me!" He put more strength into the lashes, releasing his anger on the back of my thighs as well as my ass.

"I'm sorry!" I cried. God, would he ever stop hitting me?

"I'm a bastard, Kayla—don't fool yourself otherwise." I heard the belt buckle hit the floor, and neither of us moved.

"I know what you are, Master." A walking contradiction. So were my feelings for him.

"Good. Now call your daughter before I change my mind." He stomped from the room and slammed the door upon his exit.

Exhaling a long breath, I dialed the hospital from memory. Guilt lanced through me at the sound of Eve's voice. She cried, wanting to know where I was. I held my breath and sought composure. I'd give anything to be with her, and as I recalled how effortlessly Gage had made me forget everything, if only for a while, my self-loathing intensified. I hung up after her doctor assured me she was doing okay—the only thing bothering her at the moment was how much she missed her mother. All things considered, I had to find the silver lining; the new treatment seemed to be helping.

I paced Gage's bedroom, taking in the furnishings for

the first time. The bed and dresser overpowered the room with mahogany-toned masculinity. Unlike the crimson of his basement, this room had been decorated in shades of brown, complemented with touches of royal blue. I eyed the breakfast tray. I didn't have an appetite, but I forced down what I could. A half hour had passed, and he still hadn't returned. I was completely naked, my dress lying in tatters on his floor. Wringing my hands, I went over my options for my next move. Did he want me to leave the room and find him? Or was I supposed to wait here? Not knowing what else to do, I sank to my knees and waited.

Eventually, he pushed open the door. I let out a breath of relief at the sight of him. My knees ached to a point that was unbearable.

"How long have you been waiting on your knees?"

"A while, Master."

The corner of his mouth turned up. "You know how to behave when you want to."

"Can I get up now, Master?"

He held out a hand. "Yes. You have chores to get to." He pulled the nipple clamps from his pocket. "Present your breasts."

I almost begged for mercy, but in the end I stood up straight, clasped my hands behind my back, and suffered in silence as he clamped my nipples. The passionate, lustful, *out-of-control* Gage from the night before was long gone, overpowered by a man who apparently guarded his emotions above all else.

He kept me busy with chores for hours. After dinner, he returned me to the basement, where he abused my bottom some more for his perverse pleasure. Like the previous weekend, he took me anally. Wrists and ankles locked into place on the spanking bench—a term I'd learned through my research—I was powerless to stop him as he probed my tight hole.

"Stop," I sobbed. Every last shred of composure I'd held on to vanished as he slowly inched his way in.

"It'll get easier each time we do it. Relax your muscles." It burned like hell for the first few minutes, but then Gage buried his fingers in the place he'd staked as his, and a different kind of fire erupted. "Relax," he repeated, "eventually you'll learn to enjoy it." He pushed all the way in with a hoarse groan. My body opened for him, and as he rubbed me to pleasure, my cries took on the sound of ecstasy. His body owned me, demanded my surrender, and with a smack to my crimson bottom, he commanded my orgasm. Completion crashed over me, like a tsunami that couldn't be stopped. He held his own orgasm at bay for a long time, forcing me to release twice more before he withdrew from my ass.

"Sweet dreams, Kayla," he whispered after he'd unfastened the restraints. The door to the basement clicked shut. I remained on the bench for a while, replaying what had just happened in my head. Not only had he made me enjoy it, but he'd brought me to orgasm three times. The realization stunned me, yet on some level I realized it shouldn't have. Gage had slowly knocked down my defenses, gaining compliance, and if my heart didn't yield to his intrusion, my body sure as hell did.

Again and again, whether I liked it or not.

I fell into bed and questioned my very being. What was wrong with me? What kind of person enjoyed being forced like this? How could I enjoy anything in life—least of all something so sinfully twisted—while my daughter fought for her life in the hospital? Tears trickled onto my pillow as sleep pulled at the edge of consciousness. My last thought before I fell asleep was how I'd need to find a good therapist after Gage was finished making me his plaything.

18. BETRAYING THE DEMON

The biggest surprise on Sunday was how quickly the day flew by. Gage kept me busy with additional chores, three more rounds of sex, and even the absurdity of a board game. You haven't played Scrabble until you've done it naked with a sadist who makes up his own rules. The only words allowed in Gage's rulebook were those of a sexual nature, and his prize for winning was a blow job.

Now I stood in the foyer, but unlike last Sunday, I didn't hold fast to any grand illusions of freedom. Gage's dominance would follow me out the door. He molded his body to mine from behind, one hand palming my breast as the other fell on my thigh. The hem of my dress inched up with his fingers. We'd just returned from dinner, and now the time for us to part had arrived.

Until the following morning when I'd see him at work again.

He slid his hand into my panties. "You're so sexy." His mouth left a wet trail down my neck, and every flick of his tongue coiled between my thighs. Excitement ignited at the idea of him taking me in the foyer, against the wall like he had the previous weekend. I spread my legs to give him better access.

"Do you want me, Kayla?"

I nodded, my breath coming in short spurts.

"Who am I?"

"My Master."

"You want your Master's cock inside here?" He stroked my opening, then dipped a finger into that pleasurable place.

My head fell back against his shoulder. "Yes, Master."

"I'm not going to give you what you want right now." He rubbed a circle around my clit. "And you know the rules—no masturbation. If you want it badly enough, come to me on your lunch hour tomorrow and beg for it." He gripped my hair, holding my head in place. "Is that clear?"

"Yes, Master," I breathed.

He helped me into my coat, and then he relinquished my purse and cell phone. "I was impressed by your research paper, by the way. You've learned a lot, and your behavior has showcased it." He whirled me around and pulled me against him. His mouth descended, and we said goodbye with a long slide of tongues.

"See you tomorrow at work." He opened the door for me, and I stepped into the late evening winter chill. As I hurried to my car, I felt the weight of his stare and almost looked back twice. Only after I'd slid into the driver's seat did I allow my gaze to linger on him. His eyes never strayed as I backed down the driveway. The notion was naive, but I couldn't help but smile as a sense of freedom settled over me. Freedom to see Eve. I couldn't wait to hold her. Visiting the hospital didn't take long, as it was late and Eve was tired, but I did get my cuddle time in and was relieved to find some color in her cheeks for the first time in weeks. Apparently Ian had taken my request to be left alone seriously—there'd been no sight of him, not even a quick passing in the halls as I left.

So I was stunned to find him waiting for me in my driveway, especially since I hadn't told him where I lived.

"You shouldn't be here!" I shouted the instant I exited my car. Swift anger rose until it burst free—anger at Gage for making my life so damn complicated, and anger toward Ian for making me want something I'd made myself give up years ago. I remembered in vivid clarity all the times we'd sat thigh-to-thigh on the couch watching movies during college, or how he'd wrapped his body around mine, holding on as I cried. His mere presence had been enough to set my head spinning back then; now was no different, despite the passing years.

Despite my crazy circumstances of which he knew nothing—and could know nothing—about.

I halted a few feet in front of him and crossed my arms. My angry display didn't deter him. He narrowed the short distance, standing close enough to make me high off the spicy scent of his cologne.

"I shouldn't be here? Or you don't want me here? There's a big difference."

I studied his white sneakers, jarred by how easily he sliced through my defenses with calm patience.

He tilted my chin up. "Tell me to leave...tell me you feel nothing for me, and I'll never bother you again, I promise."

I blinked several times, hating how Gage had turned me into a blubbering, crying female. I hadn't cried this often in years. Not since Rick had pushed and beat until the tears flowed, until he'd known he had the power to pound on me just as easily with hurtful words as he did his fists. "I can't tell you that." My voice cracked, as did my self-control. He opened his arms, and I fell into them.

"What's going on, Kayla? I've been trying to get a hold of you all weekend. I wanted to apologize, but you wouldn't answer your phone, and you haven't been at the hospital..." He inched back and looked at me. "You've had me really worried."

"I'm fine."

"No, you're not. Is it Rick? I saw him at the hospital Saturday."

His words turned my blood to ice. "What?" I gripped his shoulders as panic took hold of me. "Rick was there?" Impossible. He'd been arrested twice already for violating the restraining order. I hadn't seen or heard from him in over a year—I'd figured he'd finally gotten the message.

Ian opened his mouth, appearing to struggle for words. "I...I always got the impression he didn't treat you good, but you wouldn't talk to me, and then you moved and changed your number, and when I did manage to track you down, he made it clear you wanted nothing to do—"

"Wait—you came to see me? When?"

"About three years ago."

I shuddered. Rick's rage made more sense now. The final and last beating had been the most brutal, and he'd almost killed me in the end. "Let's go inside. It's freezing out here."

"I wasn't sure you'd let me in."

"I wasn't planning to, but I've already broken the rules—" And now I'd said too much; going down that path would lead straight to the subject of Gage's contract.

Ian shut the door. "What rules?"

"My rules," I said quickly. "I don't want complications in my life right now. Eve is the only one who matters."

"Of course she is," he whispered, and I suddenly found myself between him and the door. He encased me in his arms, and his breath drifted across my face as he leaned in. "She's your daughter. But you're a horrible liar, Kayla. You about shatter every time I see you. You're nervous all the time, constantly looking over your shoulder."

I was? I thought I'd hidden my inner turmoil better than that.

"Is Rick harassing you? How bad was it?"

I focused on his mouth, because looking into his eyes hurt too much. "Bad. Really bad."

He dropped his forehead against mine. "I should've done something. I suspected he was controlling, and you'd mentioned how possessive—"

"Going back to him was the worst mistake of my life."

"Letting you go was the worst mistake of mine." He

dipped his head, and I stilled, barely breathing.

"Don't."

"Why?"

"Because I'm not free to be with you right now." I was terrified. Ian and I were about to cross a line. He was a part of my past, a place where he should stay. And me? I was enslaved—literally—to a man who liked to play with my head.

"Kayla, talk to me."

I gripped his waist, wanting to keep him close even though I needed to send him packing. "I can't. You need to go."

"Like hell I do." His mouth claimed mine, and he assaulted me with the kind of hair-tingling kiss that meant something. His hands were everywhere, pulling me close at the small of my back, tangling in my hair, palming my breasts. His erection strained against my stomach, and I tore my mouth from his with a small cry.

"Stop." This was impossible. I couldn't do this.

But then I was kissing him again. He groaned and hoisted me against him. I wrapped my legs around him, and our clothing provided the only barrier between us.

"Shit, Kayla…" He buried his face in the hollow of my shoulder and moved against me.

"Ian…stop."

"Don't ask me to stop…please don't." He fastened his mouth over mine again, silencing my protests.

I was in a daze until the feel of his hands on my thighs evaporated the fog. I pushed him away, hard enough to make him stumble. "I said stop!"

His expression crumbled, and he slid to the floor, holding his head in his hands. "I'm sorry."

Shame, swift and intense, clung to me like Ian's scent did. How could I go from wanting Gage to wanting Ian in the space of two hours? What kind of person had I become? Gage would know. There was no way I could hide this from him.

"I'd never force you…this isn't like me."

I wanted to say it wasn't like me either, but I guess there wasn't much I hadn't done now, thanks to the man who'd placed metaphorical shackles around my ankles.

He looked up, and his eyes were brighter than usual. "Please, say something. God, I hate that I made you cry."

And that did me in. I fell to my knees and let him pull me against him. I let it all go—the confusion, guilt, and fear. It'd been a long time since someone cared. Of course, that only made me cry harder, but I did it in the shelter of his embrace, and a small part of me pieced itself back together again.

19. FOUR'S A CROWD

Going to work made me a nervous wreck, and it didn't help my mental state when I couldn't find my journal. That was just what I needed—punishment to compound punishment. I went through the normal morning ritual of placing his coffee on the desk, and then I pulled out my iPad. I couldn't meet Gage's eyes as he delegated the morning tasks. I avoided him as much as possible until lunchtime, when he called me into his office.

"Lock the door."

I obeyed and stood before him, eyes downcast, feeling as if my disobedience was a flashing sign on my forehead; withholding this from him all morning was eating me alive.

I have to tell him…

"Is something wrong?" he asked.

I nodded. "I need to tell you something, Master, but I'd rather not tell you here. Can I come to your place tonight?"

He tapped his fingers on the desk, and when I found

the courage to face him, his eyes had darkened to indigo. "Why don't we just get this over with now? Your punishment can wait until tonight, but you need to be upfront with me."

I bit my lip. "You're going to be angry."

"Angry doesn't describe it, Kayla." His mouth flattened into an unforgiving line. "You forgot your journal at my house last night. I drove to your place to drop it off."

My body went cold, and I folded myself into my arms, as if I could simply disappear into them. "You saw?"

"I expect you on my doorstep at nine. In the meantime, you need to get out of here before I explode."

I scampered from his office and made myself scarce for the rest of the day. That evening I spent as much time as possible at the hospital, playing a memory card game with Eve. The only bright point in my day was how much healthier she looked. I kissed her goodnight and left shortly after eight-thirty. I wasn't about to arrive at Gage's a second late.

The instant he opened the door, I threw myself at his feet. "Please, Master, forgive me." I planted my sweaty palms on the floor and studied the varying colors in the hardwood. Several seconds ticked by—seconds that seemed more like minutes. I held my breath and counted every beat of my heart.

"Look at me."

I raised my head. Tears spilled over, and no amount of willpower would stop them. Dread roiled in my stomach, and I knew with absolute certainty I wouldn't get a smidgeon of mercy from him.

"Did you have sex with him?"

"No, Master."

He narrowed his eyes. "But you wanted to."

I paused at his tone; he sounded much too confident. "Yes, Master."

"Get up."

I scrambled to my feet, limbs shaking, and bowed my head. "I'm sorry, Master. Please forgive me."

He grabbed my hand. "Come."

"Are you going to punish me, Master?" Stupid question. Punishment was inevitable; it was the way in which he planned to carry it out that worried me.

"Yes." He was too calm. He'd shown more reaction at innocent things, like when Tom had asked me out at work, or even when the waiter had smiled at me. Gage's cool demeanor was more terrifying than his rage. I wanted to turn and bolt for the door, but entertaining the notion of escape was an impossible temptation I couldn't succumb to. Like the dutiful slave he'd turned me into, I didn't fight him as he ushered me down to the basement.

And my world came to a grinding halt. Oh my God… I blinked several times, but Ian was still standing in front of me. He wouldn't look me in the eyes.

I fell to my knees and grabbed onto Gage's slacks. "Please, Master, *please*, I'm begging you. Don't involve him in this."

"I didn't involve him, Kayla. You did."

I gasped for air, as if he'd punched me in the

stomach. From the corner of my eye, I noticed Ian take a step toward me. He faltered when Gage raised a hand.

"Tell him who you belong to," Gage demanded, and when I didn't answer, he yanked me back by the hair.

"I belong to you, Master."

Ian sprung into motion. "You're not a fucking possession!" He closed the distance in three long strides. "Get up, Kayla. I'm taking you home."

Gage glared at him. "You said you'd cooperate, or do I need to carry out my threat?"

Ian bunched his hands. "I'll beat the shit out of you if you hurt her."

"I haven't done anything she hasn't agreed to." Gage let go of my hair.

"Is this true?" Ian asked, his eyes wandering to mine.

My face flamed under his perusal. "Permission to speak to him, Master?"

"Go ahead."

"I did it for Eve. He was going to send me to jail if I didn't."

"Jesus...that's not consent, that's blackmail."

"Technicalities," Gage said with a wave of his hand. "She'll agree to whatever I want, and what I want is to fuck her hard while you watch. If you care about her, you'll cooperate."

"Give us a minute alone," Ian demanded.

"Absolutely not."

"This is bullshit! I'm going to the police."

"No!" I cried. "You can't."

"You've got five minutes," Gage snapped, "but keep

your damn hands off her, got it?" He drew my attention back to him. "Don't you dare move from your knees."

Ian waited until we were alone before he spoke. "Why didn't you tell me you were being blackmailed?"

"I couldn't." I shifted, uncomfortable with being on my knees in front of him. "I don't know how much he told you—"

"He said you embezzled money for Eve's medical bills, and in return for his…discretion…you agreed to…" He shook his head, and I said the words for him, since there was no point watering down anything in this situation.

"I agreed to be his sex slave."

"Jesus, Kayla, this is insane. We can go to the police— I'm sure they'll be able to do something—"

"No. If I do that, he won't pay for Eve's treatment. She's getting better—" I broke off, overcome with emotion. "If they stop now, she'll die."

Ian took a deep breath and closed his eyes. "I can't watch him rape you. Don't ask me to do this."

"It's not rape." My voice shook as I said the words. I'd become an expert at convincing myself of half-truths, of justifying the thin line on which I'd found myself. Now I had to do the same with Ian. "I wouldn't ask otherwise, but it's Eve…please, Ian, I know she's not yours, but—"

"Don't." He fisted his hands. "You know how I feel about you. I'd do anything for you, but this?" He shook his head, and my heart dropped. Would he ever look at me the same way again after tonight? "I can't watch him hurt you."

"You won't have to," Gage announced as he came down the stairs. "She enjoys my cock." He stood, feet shoulder-width apart, and crossed his arms. "However, I doubt she'll enjoy watching you fuck another woman." He smiled toward the top of the stairs, and the axis of my world all but shattered when Katherine sauntered into the basement. She halted at Gage's side and looked down her nose, giving me a haughty once-over.

This wasn't happening…the thought of Ian with that…that complete bitch was too much. "Please, Master, don't ask him to do this."

"I'm not, you are, and if he doesn't agree, he'll live knowing that you suffered the consequences."

Ian took a step forward. "You sick—"

"Ask him, Kayla," Gage interrupted.

"No."

He narrowed his eyes. "Seems my slave has backpedaled in her training. Yes or no, Dr. Kaplan?"

My pulse pounded through my body as Ian appeared to battle with himself. Half of me—the young girl who still loved him—wanted to scream for him to say no, but the more dominant half remained silent; maternal instinct would always win in the end.

Ian folded his arms and gave a small nod.

"Katherine, treat our guest to your services. The couch will suffice."

"My pleasure." She glided across the room and curled her hand around his bicep. "C'mon, lover, I'll show you a good time."

Ian didn't budge. He trapped me in his questioning

gaze—a silent plea in the depths of intense hazel.

I mouthed, "I'm sorry," and then blinked back tears as he let Katherine haul him over to the couch. He collapsed and dragged a hand down his face.

"Strip," Gage commanded me.

I rose to my feet and brought my hands to my blouse, going on autopilot as I unhooked the buttons. Much too conscious of Ian sitting a few feet away, I kept my eyes on Gage the whole time, hoping to catch a glimpse of the man I'd seen lurking underneath during the weekend. His face displayed only calculated focus, driven by jealousy. Out of all the mistakes I could have made, this was surely the worst, for I belonged to him and he'd accept nothing less. The blouse fell from my shoulders. I reached for the front hook of my bra and sensed Ian's gaze on my breasts, so tangibly it could have been his touch.

Gage kneeled, yanking my skirt and panties down, and I stepped outside the puddle of clothing. Tears streamed down my cheeks—a testament of lost dignity. Not that he'd left me with much to begin with.

"How does it make you feel to know he'll see who you really are?"

I almost vomited at the thought.

He pulled me against him. "Does the idea excite you?"

"No, Master."

"Do you love him?"

"You know I do, Master."

Gage turned me around and bent me over the bed. Grabbing my hair, he forced my face in Ian's direction.

"Do you think he'll still love you after I've fucked you and made you scream my name in front of him?"

Through my tears, I saw Katherine kiss her way down Ian's chest, and my heart shattered when he twisted his head away. "No," I choked.

Ian clenched his hands when Gage took me from behind, his thrusts rough and unforgiving. He whispered into my ear, "You're going to come for me, or I'll take your disobedience out on him." He buried his fingers between my legs and did what he did best.

I closed my eyes and shut off my mind to Ian's tortured expression, Katherine's smugness, and Gage's cruelty. And I did what Gage had trained me to do—I obeyed, only I imagined it was Ian pounding into me, that it was his body slick against mine as I neared climax. When I opened my eyes, the sight on the couch stole my breath in agony. Katherine's head was buried in Ian's lap, and his knuckles had gone white as he gripped the cushions. He flung his head back and groaned. Hatred rushed through my blood, every last ounce of it compelling me to rebel. I made an even bigger mistake, though I didn't delude myself into believing I did it accidentally. As Gage wrenched my head back and commanded my orgasm, I screamed Ian's name at the top of my lungs.

20. REPERCUSSION

I found Ian's car parked in my driveway when I returned home early the next morning. Maybe I should have been more alarmed, considering how our forbidden embrace had started this madness to begin with, but after suffering through an intense beating from Gage, I was numb as I struggled to make it to the doorway. Gage had obliterated any positive feelings I'd harbored for him when he'd forced Ian and me into such a sick situation. The last root of that connection withered away as he'd strung me up on my toes, whipping me for hours and showing no mercy until I'd uttered the name I'd vowed to never say. The only thing saving me from jail was the fact that "Rick" was no longer my safe word, since according to our contract, I didn't have one anymore. But Gage had honored it anyway; he'd dropped the bloodied whip before unhooking me, and then he'd fallen to his knees as I collapsed to mine.

He hadn't protested as I dressed and headed toward the stairs, and I'd left without a word.

"What'd he do to you?" Ian choked out. Redness rimmed his eyes. "I didn't want to leave you—"

"You didn't have a choice." I moved past him to my door. "You shouldn't be here. This is how it all started."

"I know…Kayla, I had to see you." His presence overpowered the small space of my front porch. "Did he hurt you?"

"Nothing he hasn't done before." Another half-truth. Gage had never been so brutal. I probably wouldn't sit for days. My arms were like deadweight, and I couldn't hide a wince as I lifted my key toward the lock. Thank God my coat sleeves hid the red marks circling my wrists. "I'm sorry I got you caught up in this." I pushed the door open and held it between us. "Please go. You're better off forgetting about me."

How could he not want to after what had happened?

"Not a chance." He shoved his way inside, kicking the door shut behind him as he pulled me into his arms. I cried out in pain, and he immediately let go, though his hands never left my shoulders as he studied me. "What did he do to you?" His voice rose with every word.

"He whipped me."

"I'll kill him." He reached for my jacket. "How bad is it?"

"Don't." I shrank away from him.

"This is my fault—" he broke off, swallowing hard. "You told me to stay away and I didn't listen."

"No, it's mine. I screamed your name…" My gaze fell to the floor, and the image of him with Katherine speared through me more painfully than the impact of

Gage's whip.

Ian grimaced. "I can't stop thinking of you bent over the bed…" Avoiding my eyes, he sucked in a breath. "I'd give anything to get that out of my head."

"I have a few memories I'd like to forget as well." Namely Katherine's loud, obnoxious moans as she rode him. Only the fact that he did it for me, for Eve, kept the hurt and anger from consuming me. Though guilt was an emotion I'd live with forever. How could I be angry with him when I was the reason he'd ended up with Katherine in the first place?

"He's going to pay, Kayla. I'll make sure of it."

"You can't go there right now. If not for him, Eve wouldn't have gotten into the trial. He's paid for everything…"

"And he's about as saintly as Lucifer himself. Kayla, I hired a PI to follow Rick."

I blinked. "Why'd you do that?"

"You unsettled me on Friday, and seeing your ex the next day was too coincidental. I know you, Kayla…you wouldn't disappear on your daughter two weekends in a row without good reason."

"What are you saying? What does Rick have to do with anything?"

"I'm saying he's been in contact with your boss a lot during the past few weeks."

My jaw dropped. "What? Why didn't you tell me this last night?"

He sighed. "I didn't know last night. The PI just called me an hour ago."

Goosebumps broke out on my arms. Gage had never given me any indication he'd known my ex. "But how… why do they know each other?" I paced my living room as my mind tried to catch up. "This doesn't make any sense."

"The only connection the PI found was a woman named Jody Palmer."

"She's a friend of mine from work—" I halted. Jody, who'd gotten me the job…who'd also known Rick.

Who had also admitted to sleeping with Gage.

"The guy I hired is still digging, but he's pretty sure Rick's been blackmailing your boss."

"Why does he think this?"

"He found records. Apparently there's been several large deposits in Rick's account that match Channing's financial statements." Ian sank onto my couch and rubbed his hands down his face. "He thinks your boss has been embezzling from his clients for years. Hopefully by the end of the day, we'll have enough evidence to take to the police. You should be able to make a deal with them."

I shook my head. "No. If I turn him in, he'll stop paying for Eve's treatment."

"We'll come up with the money for it on our own."

"He did more than pay for it. He got her in that trial in less than twelve hours." I hugged myself as the force of Gage's rage washed over me. "He's furious…he won't hesitate to undo whatever it was he did to get her in."

"Don't tell me you're gonna go back to him!" Ian sprung up from the couch. "I can't stand the thought of you anywhere near that monster."

"I'm not going back to him." I met his eyes and an

idea formed—a way out that wouldn't hurt my daughter's progress. "But he no longer holds all the cards. I think it's time Gage Channing got a taste of his own medicine."

21. CONFRONTATION

Power was an interesting thing. It rose in me now, spurring me forward and stomping down the timid, scared woman Gage had molded with his thirst for domination. I clutched the manila folder—the source of my salvation—in one hand and knocked on his door.

No answer.

I pounded harder, using enough force to bruise my knuckles. The bastard was going to face me. After everything he'd put me through, he owed me that much.

"Open the door, Gage! I know you're in there!" Another few seconds of blatant knuckle abuse passed, and I finally yanked on the handle, surprised when it turned. The evening shadows darkened his foyer, but not so much as to hide the destruction of his home. I halted, stunned as the scene in front of me gave an alarming visual. Overturned furniture littered the space, picture frames had been knocked from the walls, and glass was strewn across the hardwood floor. My sneakers crunched on a piece of lightbulb as I took a cautious step into the living room. The area opened into the kitchen, which didn't look much better. Several dishes lay in pieces, and one of the cabinets had a gaping hole in the dark wood.

"Gage?" Silence greeted me—an unsettling void that raised the hair at my nape. The urge to flee was strong. I was stupid for coming, especially after what he'd done the night before, but I wanted to shove what Ian had found down his throat and see him cower for a change.

A quick scan of the dining room revealed empty space. After finding the same in his bedroom, I moved on from the sight of his bed—from the memory of the night we'd spent there—and stopped at the basement's entrance. The door stood wide open, like a cavernous mouth inviting me into the bowls of hell. I flicked on the light to chase the darkness away, and then questioned my sanity as I descended the stairs. The basement didn't fair much better than the rest of his house. His collection of whips and paddles were scattered across the floor, and the St. Andrew's cross had been torn from the wall.

"Go home, Kayla."

I clenched my jaw and closed the distance between us. Looking down, I realized two things: he was still wearing the same clothes from the previous evening, and this was the first time Gage Channing had ever sat at my feet. He kept his head bowed toward the bottle of rum clutched between his hands.

"I'm not going anywhere until I've said this." I threw the folder at his feet. "You'll find enough evidence in there to send you to jail for a long time."

"What evidence?"

"Proof of your embezzlement. How ironic that you blackmailed me for doing what you're guilty of yourself." I let out a bitter laugh. "Isn't this a tidy little circle we've got here? You steal from your clients, I steal from you. He blackmails you, you blackmail me." I gritted my teeth. "If I didn't have Eve to think about, I might find some humor in it all."

"Why are you here, Kayla?"

"The rules have changed." I paced a few steps before stopping in front of him again. "I'm here to call a truce. End our contract, pay for Eve's care, and I'll consider us even."

"Fine. You can go now." He tipped the bottle back and took a swig.

"That's all you have to say?" A tremor laced my voice. Dammit, I'd wanted so much to remain calm, just as cold and detached as him. He was more of a master at cold and calculating than he was a "Master" in anything else. "Look at me, Gage."

He raised his eyes, and I reached up and unhooked the buttons of my jacket. I stood before him without makeup, wearing sweatpants and a T-shirt because anything else hurt too much. My fingers disappeared under the hem, and I inched it up, removing my clothes and watching his reaction as I revealed the welts and bruises he'd left behind.

He took another swig, and something in his expression shifted from indifferent to pained as his gaze wandered over my body. My breasts and bottom had taken the brunt of his rage, but every inch of me showed evidence of his cruelty.

"Is this why you're hiding in that bottle? Did your conscience finally claw its way out of the grave?" I wouldn't look away or back down. I wanted…no, I needed him to acknowledge the line he'd crossed. I tapped my foot and waited. "Dammit, say something!"

"What do you want me to say? That I'm sorry?"

"Are you?"

He sprung to his feet, so unexpectedly that I jerked back. "I'll *never* be sorry for fucking you in front of him." He hurtled the bottle against the wall, and the sound of shattering glass competed with the warning going off in my head. I shrank away as he advanced, but he grabbed me anyway. His hands dug into the bruises and welts. "I'd do it again and again until he gouged his fucking eyes out."

"Let go, you're hurting me!"

"Then stop me." He caught me in his vise-like embrace, and his mouth crashed onto mine, his tongue infusing my taste buds with the bitterness of rum. I struggled until every ounce of strength seeped from my bones. Finally giving in, I sagged against him and submitted my mouth.

He tangled his hands in my hair and tilted my head back, and I was helpless against the lure of him, split down the middle between logic and need.

With a groan, he pushed me away and staggered back a few feet. "Go home, before I fuck you again, and no amount of crying or begging will stop me."

"Why are you holding back now?" My voice cracked.

"What's so different?"

He collapsed to the floor and buried his head in his hands, and he said nothing. I told myself I hadn't glimpsed a seed of remorse in his expression, that he was an ice cube underneath all that anger, incapable of feeling anything real. Problem was…I didn't believe it. I'd been ready to let his actions shatter whatever I might have felt for him, but then I'd walked into his disaster zone and seen the image of a broken man.

"If there's a speck of humanity in you, Gage"—I reached up and removed the collar—"you'll do the right thing."

The thin strip of leather drifted to the floor, and still, he said nothing. I dressed, and his silence followed me up the stairs and out the door.

22. DROWNING

I couldn't remember the last time I'd gotten drunk, but that's exactly what I was, and the culprit was a continuous supply of some fruity drink I found too easy to consume. It was like drinking Kool-Aid, only better. Kool-Aid didn't give me this amazing floaty sensation; weightless and free. I didn't have to think or feel.

Who was Gage Channing? Who was Ian? Who the fuck was I?

A persistent hand landed on my thigh, and I had to stop and think about who it belonged to. Oh, right...the guy who'd bought me the last round of drinks. What was his name?

Kyle?

Kevin?

I settled for calling him "Guy." Did it matter if I remembered his name? Likely not. Nothing mattered, which was how I wanted it. Guy's hand inched upward, and I was thankful for the ugly sweatpants I wore. He leaned in, and his beer breath overwhelmed my senses.

"Wanna get outta here, baby?"

I shook my head and stumbled to my feet, experiencing a sudden and urgent need to use the restroom.

"Hey, darlin', where're you goin'?" he protested.

I broke into laughter and had no clue why. "The lil girls' room. You can't come."

"Aw, that's not fair…"

His voice faded as I hobbled toward the bathroom. I pushed the door open and stalled at the sight of my reflection in the mirror. I looked like a zombie from a horror flick with bloodshot eyes and traces of mascara on my cheeks…right…I'd given in to a crying jag earlier. I should've stuck with bawling; drinking only made me look like hell, and in the end it was a temporary fix anyway. Tomorrow morning I'd feel just as miserable, if not more so. But I didn't indulge in alcohol often, and if Gage Channing could drown his demons in a bottle, why couldn't I?

Why do I let him get to me?

I squatted over the toilet and considered the question. I'd been prepared for all kinds of scenarios upon walking into his house. Rage, disbelief after seeing the evidence, and even his usual smugness followed by his demands, because even though I held power in my hands, surely something like the threat of jail wouldn't cause him to back down.

I'd expected a fight, only I'd gotten my first real glimpse of remorse, and it reminded me that underneath all his complexity, Gage was still a man. I finished taking care of business and crashed through the door of the restroom. I'd hit cab status long ago, but I couldn't bring myself to regret this foolish indulgence.

"There you are." Guy pulled my body flush with his, and we fell against the wall outside the restrooms. His mouth and hands were everywhere, and my first instinct was to push him away...until I realized that I needed to know. I needed to know if someone else could spark the same all-consuming feelings in me as Gage. I pulled him closer and gripped his hair, wrapped my leg around his calf, and rubbed against the bulge in his pants. His mouth plundered mine, slick and wet and all wrong, and his body moved against me, too rough and too fast.

I shoved him away. "I can't do this."

"Sure you can."

I jerked my face away as he descended again, and he slobbered on my cheek. Lifting my knee, I blindly aimed for where I knew it'd hurt most. I must have found my target, because he struggled for air. I slipped from his grasp, and his voice sounded odd as he called after me. I ignored him. In fact, I ignored everyone. Keeping my head bowed, I headed for the exit. He didn't follow. Maybe he figured I wasn't worth the trouble. And I wasn't. I wasn't worth anything. Not after what Gage had turned me into.

His whore.

Icy air hit me as I stumbled from the bar, though it was exquisite relief to my flushed cheeks. The sidewalk spun, and the brick wall of the bar blurred in my peripheral vision, as if I'd entered a funhouse...except the word "fun" didn't exist in this carnival. I fell into the wall and pounded my fists against the rough texture of the brick. Who was Gage, that he could propel me to hit bottom like this? The pain in my knuckles failed to register, and that was my problem; I was attracted to things that hurt me, even now in the way I chose to unleash my anger. Finally spent, I slumped to the ass-numbing concrete and pulled out my cell. He was the last person I wanted to face…and the one I needed to.

He'd come; I knew he would.

Ian pulled up twenty minutes later and hurried to where I sat on the deserted sidewalk. "Are you okay?" He helped me to my feet, and his gaze fell to my hands. "What happened?"

"I'm drunk."

"I can see that."

"The wall pissed me off."

"You really did a number on your hands." He put his arm around me. "Come on, I'll take you home."

I tripped over my feet and grasped his jacket. "I don't wanna go home." My empty apartment was the last place I wanted to go. "Take me home with you."

"Kayla…" His voice dropped in warning. "You need to sleep it off." He opened the passenger door of his SUV and helped me inside.

"I need you." He moved to shut the door, but I grabbed his hand and laced our fingers together. "Make me feel something."

"Not while you're drunk." He extracted his fingers from mine, and the door slammed with an echo of finality. I settled into the seat with a sigh as he rounded the vehicle.

"I went to see him," I said as he slid in beside me.

"I thought we agreed you wouldn't go alone."

"No, you *told* me not to go alone."

"How did he take it?"

"He was drunk."

"That seems to be a theme tonight." He ran a hand through his short, brown hair. "Are you all right? He didn't hurt you, did he?"

"He kissed me." Why was I telling him this?

His fingers tightened around the steering wheel. He turned onto the road and stomped on the gas. "What did he tell you?"

I laughed. "Absolutely nothing."

We fell silent, and I stewed the whole way to my apartment. He deposited me on the doorstep and straightened my jacket collar, as if I was a wayward ribbon on a present that needed fixing. Too drunk to unlock my own door, he did it for me. Nothing but loneliness and despair awaited me on the other side.

"I'll come back in the morning and take you to get your car."

"Don't leave." I gripped the front of his jacket, willing him to come inside, though I hadn't thought much on what we'd do once we got past the door. "Please, don't go." I collapsed into his arms and sobbed, body shaking violently as I let it all pour out of me. "I'm such a mess. He fucked me up, Ian." Gage was still in my system, a parasitic itch I still wanted to scratch. He'd wanted to own me, and now he did. Underneath the fear, the hatred and rage, lurked a sense of gratitude. He'd saved my daughter's life…how could I hate anyone who'd done that?

I gulped in mouthfuls of air, but it wasn't enough to calm me. Hesitantly, he tightened his arms around me, and I sensed him battling with himself. He closed and locked the door, decision made. My heart skipped as he picked me up, but then he set me on my feet next to the couch.

"No, take me to bed."

"Kayla—"

"Just hold me," I interrupted. "Please. I want to wake up with you tomorrow morning." I wanted the warmth of his body next to mine, then maybe Gage wouldn't haunt my dreams while I slept.

He cursed under his breath and lifted me again, and the last thing I recalled as my head sank into the pillow was the safety of his arms surrounding me.

23. DREAM

The gentle way he touched me bespoke of reassurance. His fingers glided along my skin, igniting want and need in their wake. He pushed a little deeper, past the resistance of my innocence and into the center of my heat, and I knew I was dreaming…dreaming of the night Ian made love to me for the first time. The one and only time.

I cried out, overcome by him filling me, pressing into me, devouring me. Never before had I dreamed so vividly in life-like detail. His skin slid against mine, hot and damp, and something beyond the physical touched me. Maybe it was the way he trembled as he grasped my hands and held them to the mattress, as if he needed to hold on to something to keep from coming apart. We hadn't needed words. The brush of our lips, the tender union of tongues, the claiming sensation of his thrusts— the way we came together said more than words ever could.

The dream evaporated, and as the light of day seeped

behind my lids, I recalled how the morning after—so many years ago—I'd ended up puking. I'd puked every morning after that for a few weeks. My eyelids fluttered open, the dream still a tickle at my conscious mind, and he was looking straight at me. The previous evening came flooding back. Oh my God…had I really begged him to take me to his place? Or even worse…had I let some random stranger stick his tongue down my throat?

"I'm sorry about last night. I shouldn't have called you." I should have called a cab and fallen into bed alone, but now here we were, seven years later.

"Don't apologize for calling me. I'm glad I was there. You weren't exactly in the best part of town."

I avoided his eyes and inspected the nasty scrapes covering my knuckles. "I was in a bad place, and I'm not talking about the area of town."

"You don't deserve what he's done." He rolled to his back and sighed. "I wish I knew what to say or do, but I don't. I don't know how to handle this…"

The memory of what Gage had put us through hit me square in the chest, and I wondered if the impact would ever lessen with time. If I could withstand the humiliation of that, then last night shouldn't bother me. "We should talk about it."

"I know."

I didn't know what to say either. He'd basically been raped—if not by force, then by threat—and I couldn't help but obsess over the fact that he'd managed to reach orgasm with Katherine. That alone was messed up on so many levels, as I'd learned firsthand how someone could coax pleasure from an unwilling participant if they put some effort into it. I closed my eyes, but the memory of them together still burned like a scorching brand on my mind and heart. His torment had shone from his gaze, but then he'd shuttered his expression and had moaned right along with her, if only for a moment.

"I don't want you to feel ashamed about it, Kayla."

Had he pretended it was me? Maybe that was the one question I wanted answered, only I didn't know how to ask, so I remained silent.

"I hate that you paid the price for saying my name, but I don't think I would've been able to…do what he demanded if you hadn't." He rolled over and faced me, close enough to breathe the same air. "I thought of you and that was enough to send me over the edge. I want you to know I wasn't with her—every part of me was with you."

I couldn't resist kissing him. To hell with the consequences, to what was right and wrong. Getting involved with him was cruel and irresponsible, but I couldn't fight the draw of him. He was my safety net, and I was falling headfirst toward concrete.

I hoped he was strong enough to catch me, because in that moment I was fresh out of strength.

For a few stolen moments, we lost ourselves in each other, our mutual moans the only sounds louder than my thumping heartbeat. Trapped underneath his body, I found freedom. We finally came up for air, and he dropped his forehead against mine.

"Kayla…" His breath caressed my lips, and I parted

them, wanting more of him. "I want you so badly right now."

"I want you too. That hasn't changed from last night."

He closed his eyes. "But sobriety has brought back reason."

Sobriety had brought back a lot of things. "Yeah." If we gave into our desire now, I might never know for certain, and I couldn't move on with him until I knew it was for the right reasons.

My phone buzzed on the nightstand, and one glance told me it was Gage. I questioned why I didn't just ignore the call—I had called in sick for a few days, after all. But the reasons were complicated, a mess of convoluted truth I didn't want to deal with. Power still tipped in his favor; in the way I submitted to him, in the way I was compelled to answer simply because he called. And with four terse words that formed a demand, he had me sliding out of bed.

"Come into the office."

24. CHECKMATE

Ian wanted me to quit my job. He had driven me to get my car, but then he'd had to go to work. I still recalled the apprehension on his face, even now as I approached the fifth floor of Channing Enterprises. He had pleaded with me not to go.

Gage Channing is a monster.
He'll only hurt you again.
At least let me go with you.

I'd agreed with the first two statements, but I wouldn't let him take time off from his job to deal with my problems. He'd been dragged into my life enough already.

A ding announced the fifth floor, and as the doors slid open, I wondered what Gage wanted. After his non-reaction to the evidence I'd presented him with, I was more than curious. Maybe he was going to fire me. A part of me hoped he would so I wouldn't have to face the decision of whether or not to put in my resignation. The idea of searching for a new job was a daunting one, though staying on as his personal assistant didn't sit well either.

I exited the elevator, not at all recovered from Gage's beating or my bar excursion, but at least no one would tell by looking at me. I wore my usual heels and skirt ensemble, only the inches on my shoes were shorter and the hem of my skirt longer than his more recent requirements. I looked like the put-together woman I wanted the world to see. No one would know that every inch of my body still ached from the impact of his whip.

"Good morning, Kayla." Katherine's sing-song greeting iced my blood. I avoided her smug face and rushed into Gage's office without knocking. The door slammed shut behind me, making him jump.

"I'll have to call you back," he said into his cell. He ended the call and leaned back in his chair, staring at me, though instead of his usual cocky air, his face was bathed in uncertainty.

I hadn't expected uncertainty. "I was debating whether or not to put in my resignation, but I can't work here with Katherine." How interesting that his presence didn't bother me half as much as hers did.

Pinching the bridge of his nose, he closed his eyes, and I assumed he was suffering from the effects of his drinking binge. "I'll have her transferred. I can't fire her— she and I have an agreement."

I bet. "Let me guess, her job back in exchange for destroying me?"

He ignored my scathing question and gestured to the seat in front of his desk. "Sit down. We have a few things to discuss."

"I'll stand, thank you. And you're the one who needs to do the talking. Why is my ex blackmailing you? Is he doing it for money, or does it have something to do with me?"

"He thinks he can keep me away from you," he said with a smirk. "Your ex is an ass."

"A bit hypocritical, don't you think?"

His face darkened, and he rose and rounded the desk.

I took a step back, remembering how he'd kissed me last night. "Don't come any closer."

"What do you think I'm gonna do, Kayla? Bend you over my desk and put a belt to your ass?" He had me against the door before I was able to blink. "You made it clear the rules have changed, remember?" His eyes lowered to my trembling mouth. "Only I'm a little unclear on what they are now. Am I still allowed to touch you?" He feathered his fingers across my nipples, as if testing how far he could push me. "Kiss you?" His words whispered across my lips, breath laced with the richness of coffee. "You didn't seem to mind last night."

"No, you don't get to touch me." I shoved him back a few inches, hating how he still had the power to make my pulse race. The bastard still turned me on; that out of everything pissed me off the most.

"I called you in here to negotiate my own terms."

I raised a brow. "I didn't realize you had anything left to negotiate with."

He laughed. "You didn't quite achieve checkmate yet —my king is still in the game, believe me."

I flattened myself against the door, but it didn't give me the distance I wanted. His chest felt like steel under my hands as I pushed against him. "I'll scream."

"Do it, then the cops can come and arrest you." His grin was too triumphant, and I wondered how he'd so easily turned the tables on me.

"And you think the police will ignore your embezzlement? You're not above the law, even though it's clear you think otherwise."

"You won't turn me in."

"Really? What makes you so certain?"

"Because upon further investigation, the Feds will discover that your friend Jody Palmer is also guilty. If I go down, she does too."

My jaw went slack. "You're lying."

"Am I? Do you want to test me?" He quirked an eyebrow. "Why do you think she resigned?"

A chill traveled through my body. He was basically telling me I had no leverage. Oh my God…this wasn't over yet. "Gage, don't do this to me. I can't take anymore."

Something flickered in the depths of his eyes, something that gave me hope, but he dashed it with the words he whispered against my ear. "Doing the right thing isn't in my nature. I want you." He grabbed my ass and lifted, and his erection pushed against my opening.

Where I instantly throbbed for him.

"No!" I shoved him away. "Turn me in, if you want, but I can't do this anymore."

"You'd risk your daughter's life?"

"No," I choked out. "God, you're despicable. The fact that you'd use her like this tells me everything I need to know about you."

He frowned. "Maybe you don't know me as well as you think." He returned to his chair, which shocked the heck out of me. Deep down, I'd expected him to take me right there in his office.

"Then do the right thing. Let me go."

"So you want me to let you out of our contract, but I'm supposed to keep paying for Eve's medical bills?"

"Haven't I paid enough? You've put me through hell and you know it."

"I'll do it under one condition."

His words stunned me, but then suspicion set in. "What do you want?"

The edge of his mouth turned up. "I already told you what I want."

He wanted me. "Why, Gage? I don't understand. You could have any woman you wanted."

"Not any woman," he said wryly.

And that was it. I was the forbidden fruit on the tree, though why he'd placed me into that category was unclear. If he'd approached me like a decent human being, I might have liked him. Now all he had going for him was my chemical reaction to him. It was just sex— really fantastic sex mixed with really horrific pain. "I'll ask again, *what do you want from me*?"

"I want your trust."

"Are you kidding me?"

He shook his head and stared at the scattered papers

on his desk. "I'm a jealous man, Kayla. I don't like sharing. But I admit that I went too far with you."

"Is this the part where I tell you it's okay?" I'd locked my anger away too long, and now it exploded in a rare display of fury. I stalked across the room and swiped the papers from his desk. Even his computer crashed to the floor, but I couldn't bring myself to care. "I don't like being raped, but that didn't matter to you."

He tensed, and for a moment I was sure he was going to explode. He stared at me for several long moments before speaking. "A part of you does like it, or you'd walk away right now."

I opened my mouth but nothing came out.

"Eve is getting better," he said. "I could stop paying for her care and she'd still recover." He leaned forward. "So why are you still here, Kayla?"

My mouth hung open, a dozen replies forming on my tongue, but the truth gagged me.

I didn't know why I was still there.

"Give me one more weekend. We'll leave the contract behind."

"And if I say no?"

He shrugged. "Well, if you'd rather carry out the rest of your six weeks, I guess I can punish you now for your blatant disobedience."

I clenched my teeth. "One weekend, then I'm free?"

He nodded. "One weekend, and then you're free."

25. JODY

Rain pelted my windows as I sat in my car, debating on whether or not to knock on Jody's door, but I was here so I might as well get it over with. I reached for the door handle but snapped my hand back when two people emerged from her house. The sight of Rick speared through me, and I gripped the steering wheel as the fight or flight instinct kicked in. He grabbed her in a way that was too familiar; hands gripping her hair so she couldn't move while he kissed her, his body trapping her between him and her front door. A passerby would see two people locked in a passionate embrace, but I saw it for what it was. Possession—the same kind Gage had wielded over me. He and Rick were made of the same cloth.

They finally broke apart, and the heat boiling in my stomach wasn't born of jealousy. I pitied the poor woman who fell for Rick's charm, for his crooked, boyish smile that was bright enough to disguise the viciousness lurking within him. No, it was hatred that set my blood afire; hatred for the man who'd taken my innocence and trust and had used them to shatter me. Flesh wounds heal— even the evidence of the beating Gage had issued would disappear—but the damage inflicted on the soul would last a lifetime.

Never taking my eyes off them, I dialed Ian's number.

"Hi…" I said once he'd answered. "It's me."

His sigh came over the line. "I was so worried. Why'd you ignore my calls?"

I shrugged. "I don't know." Only I did. My confrontation with Gage still lingered, as did the questions he'd asked that I had no answers to. Rick finally broke away from Jody, and I sank down in my seat as he crossed the street to where a shiny BMW was parked. If that wasn't evidence of Gage Channing's money, I wasn't sure what was.

"Are you okay?" Ian asked.

I hesitated, searching for an answer that wasn't total BS. "Okay" was difficult to define. "Yeah…I'm at Jody's. Gage said she's also responsible for the embezzlement."

"Jesus, Kayla. You can't trust anything he says."

"I know, but Rick just left her house, so something is definitely up. I'm gonna talk to her." I waited until the BMW disappeared around the corner before opening my door.

"I called the PI. He didn't find anything else." His frustration was obvious.

"Thanks for trying. I'll call you after I talk to her." I ended the call as I darted across the street, keeping my head ducked low against the rain. And then I found myself facing her much too soon. I opened my mouth, but no words came out.

"Kayla? What are you doing here?"

"I need to talk to you."

She stepped back and opened the door wide. "Come in."

"Thanks." I stepped inside, and I didn't miss the worried glance she sent down the street as she closed the door. I'd met her shortly after my wedding, and at one time we'd been close. Now there was a huge divide between us, only I hadn't realized how far apart we'd drifted until now. I hadn't realized the divide was Rick himself. There was no point in beating around the bush. "I saw you with Rick."

She swallowed hard, and her attention landed on anything other than me; the plush burgundy runner on the floor, the large poinsettia plant on the hutch in the foyer, even her own reflection in the oversized mirror. "I don't know what to say…"

"Why don't you start with the truth? Why is Rick blackmailing Gage?"

Her gaze jerked to mine. "What are you talking about?"

"Don't play dumb. I know about the embezzlement. Gage told me you were involved." I still wasn't sure if I believed him, but I had nothing else to go on.

She crossed her arms. "Gage Channing is crazy. You can't trust anything he tells you."

"How about his financial records? Should I trust those? The evidence doesn't lie, Jody. Money went into Rick's account, and it coincides with Gage's statements." I wondered how long her affair with Rick had been going on. Had she been sleeping with him while he'd been married to me? "Since I just saw Rick leave here, I'm going to assume Gage was telling the truth."

"I have no idea what you're talking about. Look, I know this must be a shock to find out about Rick and me this way, but—"

"It's more than a shock—it's crazy! Jody, do you have any idea what he's capable of?"

She pursed her lips. "It's been three years. I thought you'd be over him by now."

I was sure my eyes bulged. "You think I'm still hung up on the man who beat the shit out of me?" I took a step toward her. "How long has this been going on? Has he hit you yet?"

Jody shuffled back and wrapped her arms around herself. "He's changed. He never meant to hurt you."

I arched my brows. "Really?"

"He told me what happened. You don't have to be ashamed—a lot of women suffer from postpartum depression and do things they regret."

I stared at her, incredulous. "This should be good. Please, enlighten me—what bullshit did he feed you?"

"It's in the past." She shook her head. "I know you'd never try to hurt yourself or your daughter under normal circumstances, and obviously you got the help you needed —"

"Obviously," I snapped, folding my arms. "I can't believe you're buying into his lies."

"He wouldn't lie to me. He loves me."

I almost snorted. "Rick doesn't love anyone."

"He loves me, and he loves Eve. You can't keep him from her forever. He already lost a year and half in prison."

I blinked, struggling to form a reply to such a crazy statement. "He should have been locked away a lot longer for what he did to me." His expensive attorney had gotten him a lenient plea bargain, otherwise he'd still be in jail, and I'd still be safe from the threat of him. "How long has it been going on?" I asked.

She studied the purple nail polish on her toes. "Since before you guys split. I'm sorry. I never meant to hurt you, Kayla."

"You're going to be the sorry one. Rick is rotten underneath his appeal." I headed toward the door and opened it. "Tell him if he comes anywhere near Eve, I'll have him thrown in jail again."

Her expression iced over. "It's not fair to keep him from her. He just wants to be part of her life—we both do."

"Over my dead body." I slammed the door behind me, and Ian called before I reached my car. He started talking the instant I answered.

"I'm going on my lunch break now. Can I come over? I need to see you."

"I need time, Ian." I slid in behind the wheel and slumped in my seat. Letting him past my defenses that morning had been a mistake.

"Why do you keep shutting me out?"

"I don't want to shut you out, but…"

"But what?"

I'm ashamed.

"I've got some stuff to sort out. I'm sorry." I hung up, shut off my phone, and headed to the hospital to spend the rest of my day with Eve. And I prayed to God Ian would stick to the wing he worked in.

26. CHRISTMAS

Eve's doctor gave me the best Christmas present I could've hoped for. My baby was coming home in two weeks.

I must have cried happy tears for an hour straight, and thankfully Eve was too preoccupied with opening her gifts and visiting with Santa to notice that her mother was a basket case. Only this time I was a basket case in the best sense of the word; I hadn't been this happy in months.

So of course Gage would have to ruin my Christmas with his mere presence.

"Merry Christmas," he said, nodding toward Santa as the big guy in red and white exited Eve's room. Gage shut the door and took the empty seat on the opposite side of her bed.

I gawked at him as he began removing presents—all of them wrapped in shiny paper splashed with Santa's reindeer and adorned with fancy bows. I wondered if he'd wrapped them himself or if he'd paid the department store to do it for him. He smiled at Eve, a grin so huge and unguarded that I did a double take. When she sat up and grinned back, something within me unleashed. I bolted from my chair and pulled him away from her.

"What the hell do you think you're doing here?"

He had the nerve to look offended. "It's Christmas. What do you think I'm doing here?"

"Mommy! Can I open them?"

"Of course you can," he answered before I was able to. "I brought them especially for you."

I glared at him. "I won't let you use her to get to me. I don't want you anywhere near her." I lowered my voice amidst Eve's enthusiastic package-opening. "Do you understand? She's off-limits to your sick games. You can play them with me all you want, but you'd better leave her out of it." If I hadn't been so worked up myself, I would have been alarmed by the fury that crossed his face.

His gaze darted behind me, and I turned around and noticed Eve's curious expression. He grabbed my hand and pulled me toward the door. "I need to talk to your mom. Merry Christmas, Eve." He practically dragged me from her room, and I saw him strain under the effort it took to keep from slamming the door. He moved against me, both arms trapping me between him and the wall.

"Let me go. This is *not* the place."

"Don't you think I realize that?" He ground his teeth. "Let's get something straight *right now*." He leaned even closer and spoke to me nose-to-nose. "I would never... *never*...hurt Eve."

"You expect me to believe that after the last beating

you gave me?"

He buried his face in the hollow of my shoulder, and I felt him inhale deeply. "If I could take it back, I would."

I went still. I'd guessed he was dealing with some amount of guilt, but I never thought he'd admit it. "Why'd you do it?" I squeezed the question past my constricted throat.

"Get your hands off her."

Gage pushed away from the wall and glanced at Ian, who looked ready to greet him with his fists. "Dr. Kaplan," he said, his tone unworried. He returned his attention to me, as if Ian's presence didn't matter. "Next weekend, Kayla. I'll pick you up at seven." He brushed his lips across my cheek. "Wear something sexy." My face flamed, both from anger and embarrassment as he took off down the hall.

"What is he talking about?"

I studied the worn carpet. "He said he'd let me out of the contract if I gave him one more weekend."

"And you believe him?"

I was tired of trying to figure everyone out, of trying to understand my own reactions to a man whose presence should send me running in the opposite direction. "I don't know what to believe."

"He's gotten under your skin."

I wanted to deny it, but it'd be a lie. Gage *had* gotten under my skin, only I hadn't realized to what extent until now. Until Ian had thrown the truth in my face. Gage hadn't just cast the line; I'd opened my mouth and let him hook me.

Ian let out a curse. "After everything he's done, how can you have feelings for him?"

"I don't." I stepped back against the wall and folded my arms.

"Then why are you agreeing to this?"

"It seems like the best way out."

"You could go to the police. It's not too late."

"Not if Jody's involved." It didn't matter if she'd betrayed me as a friend. I wouldn't drag her through this situation. "It's only one more weekend, and then it'll be over."

He dropped his head. "I can't talk you out of this, can I?"

I silently pleaded for him to talk me out of it, to pull me back, because I feared Gage had me in his sights and there was nowhere to hide. Nowhere for me to go but downhill from here, and what really sucked was how familiar this path was.

So was the same sense of helplessness I felt.

His composure fell apart, and he leaned against the wall, his arm hiding his face. "This is my fault. I did this." Before I could refute or question his claim, he pushed away from the wall. "I've gotta go."

He bolted down the hall, and I felt more confused than ever.

27. FLIGHT

The week sped by too fast. Ian was obviously avoiding me, something I had to admit was a relief. Gage and I barely spoke, another source of relief. He'd kept me busy at work with tasks that kept me out of the office for the majority of the workday, and I spent my nights at the hospital with Eve.

I'd been a nervous wreck all week. I couldn't help but wonder what Gage had planned for me at the week's end, and considering how he'd chosen New Year's Eve to begin our last weekend together, I couldn't deny I was edgy…and curious.

Now as I slipped into a red halter dress, I recognized something was different about this weekend. Gage had told me on Wednesday that he was taking me out of town —not far in case Eve needed me—which only heightened the nervous flutters in my gut. I prepared my hair and put on my makeup. He hadn't even arrived yet, but I sensed it; this weekend was significant, only I didn't know why. It felt more like a date. I floundered at the thought, but I didn't have time to dwell on it. A knock sounded on the door.

The reality of his arrival trembled through me. The idea that he wanted my trust was absurd. It didn't matter how much I warred with myself—I would always remember the brutality of his hands. I took a deep breath and opened the door. He wore a dark suit, black on smoke gray, and he'd left the tie at home. He'd unfastened the top two buttons of his collar. I stumbled back a little. He looked good enough to eat, though taking a bite of that would likely poison me.

His wandering gaze heated, and I was certain he'd already undressed me in his head. "Are you ready to go?"

With a nod, I picked up the overnight bag I'd left by the door. "Where are we going?"

"You'll see." He grabbed my bag, and I shut and locked the door. Moments later we were in his car speeding down the highway, and it became apparent that we were headed to the airport.

"You said we weren't going far."

"We're not. It's only a two-hour flight on my jet. I can have you home in no time if need be."

I wasn't happy about this development, but I let it go. One more weekend, and it would be over. I was prepared to take whatever the next two days gave me. He parked next to a sleek jet where a man materialized next to the car and pulled our bags from the trunk. Gage placed his hand on the small of my back as we climbed the steps. His touch had a possessive connotation, and when he clamped his fingers around my side, I resisted the urge to squirm out of reach.

The inside of the plane was bigger than it appeared from the outside. I'd expected a few seats and little more. I should've known better. The inside was just as luxurious as everything else he owned. Every detail testified of money and power; the large flat screen television on the wall, the abstract pieces of art, the plush rug under our feet. He ushered me to the cream leather couch that spanned one side.

"Straddle me," he demanded, pulling me onto his lap and denying me the chance to object. He slid his hands under my dress and grabbed my ass, bringing me against his erection. My reaction was instantaneous. A flood of warmth crashed at my center, and I struggled to catch my breath through lips that parted of their own volition. His hands kneaded my bottom. "You feel that?" Awareness zinged between us as he watched me. "We connect here, Kayla."

"It's just sex." My voice sounded weak, and I despised myself for it, especially since my body rocked against his.

"No, you're not the type of woman who engages in 'just sex' arrangements." He brought his hands up and spanned my ribcage. "The fact that you're sitting here hot for my cock after everything I've done"—he circled my nipples with his thumbs—"turning to liquid at my touch, gives you away. You can have 'just sex' with anyone. There's more here between us."

I couldn't look at him anymore. I closed my eyes, but I still felt his hands on me, still felt him hard and hot underneath me.

"I could fuck you right now, and you'd still beg for more." He grabbed the back of my neck and pulled me in. "You're just as addicted to me as I am you." Pressing his mouth to mine, his tongue swept inside, and I wondered what he was waiting for.

"Do it, Gage." I moaned against his lips. Later I'd beat myself up for this. Later I'd walk away.

"No. Just because you're not my slave anymore, that doesn't mean you call the shots." He palmed my ass and squeezed hard. "And I'm still Master to you in the bedroom." His tone left no room for argument. Before I could argue with him anyway, he was kissing me again. He freed my hair from my up-do, and the heavy locks fell in waves around his face.

I curled my fingers in the silk of his hair, but he grabbed my hands and held them behind my back, clenched together in his strong fist. His other hand held me to him so I couldn't pull out of the kiss until he allowed it. And I didn't want to escape his mouth. We kissed long after the jet left the ground, and only a patch of turbulence severed our lips, though he didn't release me.

"Let's talk," he rasped against my cleavage.

I could hardly breathe or think, and he wanted to talk? I inched away and studied his expression, looking for a clue as to what he was thinking. "You want to talk? Now?" My head spun—from his kiss, from his rapid mood-shift.

"Yes. Talk. We haven't done much of that."

No, we hadn't. He'd always distanced himself. He

gently pushed me from his lap and patted the seat beside him. I sat, expecting him to dominate the conversation, to drill me with questions he demanded answers to, much like he had over breakfast during my first weekend with him. "What do you want to talk about?"

"You." He ran his hand along the back of the couch and played with my hair. "Why did you marry him?"

The question hit me in the gut. "Do we really have to talk about this?"

"Yes."

"Okay, but as long as you promise to be open with me. Conversation is a two way street."

"Fine."

"I got pregnant. I was young, and I thought marrying him was the right thing to do."

"Did you know he was abusive beforehand?"

"No. I mean, he was possessive, and I knew he angered easily. But he'd never hurt me before."

"Did you love him?"

I rubbed the silky hem of my dress between two fingers. "At one time, maybe I did." Raising my eyes to his, I asked, "Have you ever been in love?"

"No." His reply was too quick.

I raised a brow. "Not even a little? Most people fall in love at least once in their lifetime."

"Maybe I was waiting for the right woman." His gaze, hot and suggestive, pinned me to the seat.

I refused to back down. "So there was no one…?"

"Once, a long time ago." He said it like it was ancient history—as if this part of his past didn't mean anything, but I was certain it did mean something. I sensed that whatever happened was a factor in what had made him so deranged. Normal people didn't enjoy inflicting pain on others in the manner he did. Even the normally kinky people knew where to draw the line. Gage didn't.

"So what happened?"

"This isn't open for discussion, Kayla."

"We had an agreement. You promised to be open with me."

"I'm modifying that agreement now. Drop it."

I crossed my arms. "No."

"Are you purposely trying to make me angry? Maybe you like punishment more than you've let on."

"I like a lot of things, Gage, but pain isn't one of them. I'm asking because I want to know you. Don't you think I deserve that much, after everything you've done to me?"

He ran a hand through his hair. "You deserve everything." He turned his face toward the blackness outside the small window, contemplation shadowing his features. "She was my high school sweetheart." Several moments of thick silence passed, as if he thought those six words explained everything.

"Was she…was she your slave?"

His mouth twitched. "I never had a slave before you. She was the opposite of you. I'd whip her and she'd beg me to do it harder. She loved it."

Sounded like they were made for each other. "So what happened?"

"She was fucking someone else."

Okay…so he'd had his heart broken. Not exactly the precipice I'd been looking for to clue me in on why he was such a sadistic bastard. "And there's been no one since?" I found that hard to believe. I knew he'd had an immeasurable amount of women, but surely he'd had at least a couple of relationships.

"No."

"So she cheated on you, broke your heart, and you what? Decided to go the rest of your life hating women?"

"She died." He glared at me, and I felt every facet of that hostile gaze. "I told you to drop it."

The fear came back then, creeping up my spine, tingling along my skin and reminding me that Gage wasn't a romantic lover, this wasn't a date, and he wasn't going to whisper endearments in my ear as we made love. He'd whittled away my guard, making me forget how he could turn on me in an instant. Like a rabid dog.

"I'm sorry," I said, adverting my gaze.

He forced my chin up, though his touch was more gentle than usual. "There are things about my past you don't need to know about. I don't want you to think you can't talk to me, or ask whatever is on your mind, but when I tell you to drop something, I mean it. Understand?"

I nodded. Obviously, I'd pushed too far. If he wanted to dish out punishment now, I deserved it. In the back of my mind, I realized how skewed that notion was, but there it was.

The next hour passed in uncomfortable silence, and I couldn't help but wonder about his past, about the

174

woman who'd stolen his heart. What had happened to her? Did he hold himself responsible for her death? I shrugged off the tense silence and the questions as we began to descend. Peering out the window, I spied a neon expanse below, and the closer we got, the bigger the buildings appeared. He'd taken me to Las Vegas. I'd never been, but I recognized the infamous strip, and I'd heard how spectacular Vegas was on New Years Eve.

What the hell was he up to?

After the jet came to a stop, he rose and held out his hand. The next half-hour sped by in a blur. People opened doors as if we were royalty, and during the limo ride down the strip, the bustling atmosphere called to me, called to the flutters of excitement in my stomach.

Him bringing me here…it was beginning to make sense. He wanted to show me how good it could be at his side, but what he hadn't stopped to think about was how he'd already shown me the worst of him. No amount of seduction, sexual or otherwise, would erase that, though I had to admit I was being lured in for a weekend of the best of Gage Channing…at least I hoped he'd left the sadist at home.

After arriving at the hotel, we bypassed the registration desk and went straight to the bank of elevators off the lobby. I watched the numbers light up as we climbed upward. Of course, we didn't exit until we reached the top floor. He placed his hand on the small of my back, a touch so light that outsiders would think nothing of it. I knew better. His every touch signified ownership.

"I want to blindfold you," he said once we'd stopped in front of the door to our room.

My heart galloped ahead of me for a moment. "Why?"

"Trust me."

"You think you've earned my trust?"

"No, but I think you're going to give it to me anyway." He produced a blindfold from his pocket and reached for me.

I opened my mouth to protest, but he was already slipping it over my eyes. I felt silly standing in the hall, blindfolded while he opened the door. No one else was around to witness my compliance, but that didn't stop me from wondering about surveillance cameras. After a few moments I heard a beep, and he guided me inside.

"Watch your step," he murmured. The floor dipped, and he walked me further into the room, his hands on my hips guiding me the whole way. "Stop here."

I halted and waited, holding my breath, wondering what he'd do. I'd agreed to the blindfold but nothing else…and he hadn't mentioned anything else. I reminded myself that I wasn't under his control any longer. He'd promised no contract.

So why did I feel like this whole trip was a sham? Like I had even less freedom than I'd had before? I drew in a quick breath, and something deep inside me called to him, something craving the unknown—that tingle of anticipation mixed with fear. The part of me that fell back into the dynamic of submissive too easily. The word "Master" was on my tongue, begging to be spoken.

"Will you whip me if I call you by your name?"

"Yes."

"Will you stop if I tell you to?"

A few seconds went by, and I heard him inhale. "Yes, but I don't think you want to."

He was only partly right. I wanted to tell him to stop, but I felt as if I couldn't.

"Lift your arms," he instructed, and clearly, that line of questioning was over. Whatever he had in mind, he was ready to begin.

"Gage—" I broke off, cringing as I lifted my arms above my head. Had I slipped up on purpose? Did I want to test the new perimeters of our agreement?

He chuckled…the bastard actually chuckled. He dragged the zipper of my dress down, his fingers lighting a fire down my back. My breath hitched when he bent and placed his hands on my thighs. His fingers were close to the wetness between my legs, tantalizingly close, and I bit back a moan as the ache spread. I couldn't hold it in when his hands glided upward, palms caressing my stomach and breasts as he pushed the dress up my body and over my head. Gooseflesh broke out on my arms and traveled down my legs, and as he walked me forward a few more feet, I couldn't stop shaking.

"Cold?"

"A little."

"Brace yourself," he said, and I was clueless about what he meant until he pushed me against the cold, hard surface of what I assumed was a window. I gasped at the contact, and my nipples pebbled against the glass. I was probably visible to God knew who, naked except for a thong and heels, but I didn't care. All that mattered was the next moment...and whether he planned to unleash his sadistic or sensual side.

He grabbed my hands and placed them flat against the glass, and something soft and silky encircled my wrists. "I'm going to whip you," he said, voice gentle as the bindings tightened.

His words elicited a deep freeze in my bones, much colder than the chill on my skin, and I replayed the agony of being struck for hours in my head. I tried to jerk away from the glass, but he'd tethered my hands to something. "Master..." The name tumbled out, a plea for mercy I knew didn't exist within him. "Please, I can't take another beating like that."

"Shhh..." He swept my hair aside and placed the heat of his mouth on my neck. "I'm not going to hurt you... much." He left a wet trail down my back, and by the time he cupped my mound and slipped his fingers inside, I was dripping wet. He owned me there, with the simplicity of his touch, with the way he made my insides pulse around his fingers. Forgetting that I should be scared, I opened up for him and moaned.

"I won't lose control like I did last time." He increased his strokes. In and out...in again, slowly caressing, dipping deeper until I started humming. Sweet tension spread from my belly to my limbs, and my breasts heated against the glass, no longer cold.

I was on fire.

Holy hell...

I held my breath, knowing I was about to come, but he stopped.

"Master—"

Without warning, he shoved a gag into my mouth. "Quiet." That single word, spoken calmly but with enough warning to let me know he meant business, silenced me more effectively than the gag. I wanted to beg and plead, but I didn't dare, even though one important question screamed in my head; how could I say no if he wouldn't allow it?

"I want you to trust me," he said, as if he heard the turmoil of my thoughts. "I know I've given you no reason to, but I'm going to change that. I won't hurt you like I did last time, but I am going to punish you, and if you make a sound I'll extend the punishment." He ran his hands over my bottom. "Can you behave yourself?"

I nodded.

"Can you remain quiet?"

I nodded again but doubted my ability to obey.

"I'm giving you the chance to say no now, but once this moment passes, you're mine." He squeezed my ass, and I bit back another moan. "Shake your head if you want to say no."

Part of me pleaded with me to do it—the more logical, level-headed, self-respecting part. Just a simple shake of my head would stop this. I had power now. But what if I did…and he stopped…everything? God, I was pathetic. I wanted him so badly, I ached.

My moment of escape passed, and he stepped away. The sound of him removing his belt made me cringe, and the whoosh of that familiar strip of leather reached my ears an instant before it hit my ass. I bit down on the gag to keep silent, though the pain wasn't bad. Yet. It'd get worse; it always did. I jerked each time he struck my tender bottom and counted the lashes in my head. Fourteen…fifteen…sixteen…seventeen…

My eyes flooded with unshed tears at twenty, and by twenty-five the first drop fell. I felt dirty and worthless—much worse then ever before, because I'd allowed this to happen this time. He'd given me a choice, and I was still restrained, trapped by my body's need for him, helpless and at the mercy of his belt.

Why hadn't I stopped this? This was insane.

A whimper escaped my throat, and he stopped. "Naughty girl."

I jumped when he pulled the thong aside and inserted a small vibrator between my damp folds.

"Close your legs to hold it there. If you drop it, you won't be allowed to orgasm tonight. And you won't have my permission until I'm deep inside your ass." He swatted my bottom to make his point. "Not a sound, Kayla."

He was the devil.

I scratched at the window as he continued the lashes. In the back of my mind I realized he wasn't putting all his strength behind them. I knew how unbearable a real whipping was at his hands, and this wasn't it. But it stung like hell, and I held onto the sensation to keep from climaxing.

I wanted him. Inside me, in my mouth. I didn't care—I just wanted him, and fooling myself otherwise was a waste of time.

"Your ass is such a sexy shade of red."

Smack!

Unforgiving leather delivered punishment for several more minutes, and just when he was about to stop, I'd moan or whimper and it'd start all over again. The pain was harder to handle, more intense, as were the vibrations going through my body. Tears and sweat drenched my face, and I stood straight as a pillar, clenching my thighs to keep the vibrator in place. Orgasm teased from the outskirts, there…but just out of reach.

The pain overshadowed the pleasure.

I bit hard on the gag as the last few minutes drove me to my limits. Finally, he dropped the belt. "Keep that vibrator where it belongs." He bent me over and pushed into my ass, inch by inch, and I didn't even consider protesting.

A loud boom sounded outside, followed by another, and another…he slid in further, removed the blindfold and gag, and a guttural scream tore from my throat. I arched my spine as an orgasm washed over me—swift in the onslaught, but deliciously long in duration. The Las Vegas strip exploded in a dizzying whirl of color, and I knew the fireworks outside couldn't begin to compete with the ones between Gage and me.

28. GAMBLE

The man liked to gamble. A lot. He'd been at it for most of the day, and if I'd harbored any guilt about the amount of money he'd spent on Eve's care, I didn't now. I was disgusted at how easily he threw away his money, but I couldn't help but watch in morbid fascination. So *this* was how the other half lived. I still couldn't wrap my mind around it.

The guy next to us arranged the dice the way he wanted them. His blond hair brushed his collar, and every time he leaned forward to roll, his shirt sleeve grazed my arm. He shot a grin at me before tossing the dice toward the opposite end of the craps table. The large crowd pressed in on all sides, and everyone erupted in cheers.

"Easy six!" One of the gaming attendants said.

Gage just won some of this money back. He leaned against my back and reached in to collect. We'd been standing in this position for the past hour; him behind me, his arms caging me in and his cock nudging my ass. He'd been rock-hard the whole time, and not even the man next to us, with his bold and inviting smile, distracted Gage from his desire. I tensed every time the guy aimed his flirtations in my direction, but so far Gage hadn't unhinged.

But he was about to.

His rum-scented breath drifted across my bare shoulder, and he brought his lips to my ear. "If he looks at you like that one more time, neither of you are going to like the outcome." He pushed his erection into my left butt cheek a little harder and tightened his arm around my waist. "Quit being so damn sexy." Of course, in Gage Channing's twisted mind, this would be *my* fault.

Poker chips were dropped and picked up, clacking together in the triumph of a win, and excited chatter charged the air as everyone prepared for the next come-out roll. Mr. Big Flirt did something stupid; he touched me.

"It was all you, baby! You're my lucky charm!" His fingers circled my wrist, and he wrenched my arm up in the air, as if we were champions celebrating a win.

Oh no. No, no, no…

Gage clamped his fingers around the guy's wrist and squeezed until my hand fell free. "Touch her again, and I'll break off your fucking fingers."

The guy shrank back, his eyes going wide. I couldn't blame him. If Gage hadn't so effectively trapped me between him and the table, I would have done the same thing. I didn't have to see his face to know his features were twisted in rage.

"Dude, you need to chill out. I didn't mean anything

by it."

One of the table attendants interrupted their argument. "Is there a problem here, Mr. Channing?"

"Yes. This asshole thinks it's okay to harass and paw at my date."

And that was the last I saw of Mr. Big Flirt, though his indignation at being escorted away like a criminal lingered. Just like Tom's had at work. Hating how everyone's focus was drawn to me, I pushed away from the table. "Let me out." I cranked my neck and glared at him. "*Right* now, Gage. I'm not kidding."

He backed away, and I bolted. Tears threatened to spill over as I weaved through the multitude of gamblers. Heavy smoke drifted in the air, which only made my eyes burn more. Gage caught up to me at the elevators. We both entered, and I kept my attention fastened on the doors, unwilling to look or speak to him.

And he didn't speak to me.

I wasn't sure what was going to happen when we got back to our room, but it couldn't be good. Would he be able to see through his haze of red to hear me say no? Or was I in for another horrendous beating? Hysteria rushed up and lodged under my breastbone, and I could hardly breathe as the doors slid open at our floor. He dug his fingers into my arm and dragged me to our suite. My face was already wet with tears.

"Please, Gage—"

"Shut up."

He swiped his card, the light flickered green, and the beep signaled the beginning of what I knew was going to be a hellish night.

"I'm saying no," I said as soon as he shoved me through the door. "Wha…whatever"—I swallowed the vomit rising in my throat—"whatever you're gonna do, stop."

The door slammed, and he pushed me against it. "I said shut up." His hands shook, which only intensified the terror fisting my heart. "What I'm going to do," he said, his gaze dropping to my mouth, "is kiss the fuck out of you." He tangled his hands in my hair, leaned in, and sighed against my lips. "Do you have a problem with that?"

No, but I should have.

It was my only thought as he took control of my mouth. Hot tongues swirling together, the taste of rum on his lips, the way he moaned my name before sucking my lower lip between his teeth, and his fingers tightening in my hair, pulling against my scalp—every sensation zipped through me like a firefly. I should definitely have a problem with this.

I couldn't recall the space of time between the door and the bed, but the mattress welcomed the weight of my body, and Gage blanketed me, his mouth never leaving mine, never failing to suck the free will from my soul with the poison of his kiss. He grabbed at my dress, ripping and tearing, and his frantic fingers clutched handfuls of me; my hips, my thighs, shoving my legs wide open, pushing my knees up an instant before he slammed into me. He was like a beast, desire his claws, and I came apart under his lethal need.

"Gage!" I urged him deeper, spreading my thighs further and arching to meet him. He pressed high into me, so high all I could feel was him.

He grunted, his forearms shaking on either side as he pumped. "Who am I, Kayla?" He plunged one more time, violently, and then went still.

I met his gaze—maniacal eyes possessing me—and shuddered. My heart feared him, but the gate of my sexual need was manned by him, owned by him.

And he knew it.

"Say it, or I'll stop right now and cuff your hands to the headboard. I'll make you edge all night until you're begging me to fuck you."

"Master." I tilted my hips upward. "You're my Master. Don't stop."

With a growl, his body engulfed mine, smothering and consuming, and the only thing more painful than being devoured so thoroughly was the sound of my unrestrained moans, a traitorous testimony of his control over me. My need for him ripped from my throat and poured from my being with every thrust.

And then I was chanting his name. "Master… Master…Master…" Moaning and moaning and moaning. "Master…Master…Master." More moaning, more thrusting…and he was getting off on every sexual plea.

I was getting off on *him*.

I dug my nails into his shoulders and scratched my unbridled desperation down his back, on the cusp of splintering. It was right there for the taking—and with stunned frustration, I realized why my body wasn't shattering.

I was waiting for his permission.

"Let me come, Master."

He groaned. "Say it again. Tell me how bad you want it."

I grabbed fistfuls of bedding, and a pitiful, keening cry broke loose. I rose to meet him, again and again, and gasped my plea. "Please! Give me permission, Master!"

He groaned again, an unrestrained sound that vibrated to my core. "Fuck, woman, I'm never letting you go." He gripped my head and forced my gaze to his. "Come for me."

I fell into oblivion.

His sapphire eyes drank me in as I came undone, holding me prisoner in their depths until the last wave carried me to a place only he could send me. I was gasping, struggling just to breathe, when his control began to slip. I watched him in wonder, in awe by the raw pleasure twisting his features. We'd never been so close as we were in this moment; he'd never allowed himself to go like this, had never allowed me to see it. He buried himself to the hilt, and his forehead fell against mine.

"Kayla…" He squeezed his eyes shut and moaned. "Baby…"

I buried my hands in his hair, fingers brushing the sweat at his nape. The sound of his vulnerability was the sexiest thing I'd ever heard. He cried out, hoarse and powerful, sensual and conquering, a sound of unstoppable release that poured out of him as he spilled into me.

29. LION'S DEN

Gage gave me the ultimate Vegas experience on our last night in Sin City. Cirque du Soleil, a ridiculously expensive dinner at Guy Savoy—even a helicopter tour at nightfall. He was the epitome of charm, from the way he opened doors for me to the way he guided me with a hand to the small of my back. All the women we came in contact with flirted with him, and he fooled them all into believing the facade.

He'd even fooled me, for a while. But then we'd boarded his jet, and he'd reverted back to the same old Gage by pushing to me to my knees. And I hadn't protested. I'd grown wet between my legs as I swallowed every last drop of him. That was how he'd left me on my doorstep—hot and wanting him, despite the chilly late night air. With one final kiss, a quick brush of his lips to mine, he'd disappeared from my life. Just like that.

That had been two weeks ago.

He'd transferred me to another department the week following our trip, and there'd been no phone calls or demands. He hadn't sought me out once, other than to send a copy of our voided contract. Now I was a bewildered mess because his actions disappointed me. I couldn't explain it—this hollow in my chest he'd left behind. I wanted my freedom, and I still despised him for the way he'd hurt me, but…

I missed him. I missed the way he consumed me, missed the way he sent me crashing into deep space. I thought about scheduling an appointment with a shrink, but the thought of divulging the cause of my stress humiliated me too much. He'd used and abused me, and now that he'd let me go, I couldn't stop thinking about him.

And all the while, Ian stood by, kind, understanding, and displaying the patience of a saint. He'd stopped by every day to see me—at the hospital, at home, even after work. But we didn't talk about it. Gage sat between us, an unspoken entity. My horror at what I'd done—at how easily I'd succumbed to my desire for Gage—made me keep Ian at arm's length.

I wiped the unsettling thoughts from my mind as the elevator approached the fifth floor. The doors slid open, and as a tall brunette entered, I let the tension slowly seep from my body. The doors narrowed toward the center, but a black dress shoe stopped them from completing their slide. Gage's eyes met mine. I sought the farthest corner and tried to fold myself into it—obviously my body understood the threat he represented, even if my heart didn't, and my heart was beating like a caffeinated little drummer boy.

The elevator stopped at the third floor where the woman got off and left Gage and me alone. The air was instantly stifling, heavy with fear and the undeniable spark of sexual tension. I jumped when he moved and studied my shoes upon the funny look he gave me.

"How's Eve?"

"She's good. They're letting her come home tomorrow."

A smile broke out on his face—one so rare I wanted to snap a picture just to have proof that Gage Channing was capable of such a grin. "I'm glad." The doors opened into the parking garage, and without another word, he exited.

I puzzled over the strange encounter as I approached my car, heels tapping an echo through the deserted garage. Gage backed out of his spot and disappeared through the exit, and as I opened my car door, a voice from behind stopped me cold. I jumped and whirled.

Jody stood there, sporting two black eyes and a busted lip.

"Rick's been drinking again." Her mouth trembled, and like a scared child, she folded her arms around herself. "He really had changed, Kayla. He was doing so good." She dropped her arms to her sides and formed two tight fists. "But you kept him away from Eve, and now he's going crazy. Why'd you have to be such a bitch?"

I slammed my door. "Don't you dare put this on me. He's dangerous." I shook my head. "I thought we were friends, Jody. Let me help you."

Her bitter laughter bounced off the walls of the

garage. "Friends? We haven't been friends in a long time. Why, Kayla?"

"I-I don't know. Eve got sick…" And I'd checked out on life for a while. I'd lost touch with everyone. "I'm worried about you."

"Well don't. Just quit provoking him already." She took off toward a bright red Honda parked nearby. The tires screeched as she slammed on the gas and raced through the exit.

Her words percolated in my head all evening, an unwanted distraction that intruded on my time with Eve. I tossed and turned next to her for hours after she fell asleep, unable to stop thinking about my encounters with both Gage and Jody.

It was past midnight when I found myself in his driveway. I needed to figure out why he drew me to him like a magnet, regardless of how much he hurt me… would always hurt me. People didn't change, and I wasn't about to kid myself otherwise. He'd always be the same sadistic bastard with a taste for my pain. I shut off the ignition, and the utter quiet of the night surrounded me. Haunted me. Ghosts weren't so easily laid to rest in the still of the night.

Why am I here?

I had no answer—none that made any sense. He'd let me go. I was free…yet here I was walking into the lion's den. My limbs quaked as I approached his door, and I almost turned back. I told myself to turn back, even chanted the words in my mind over and over again as if doing so would be enough to convince me. My traitorous fist wasn't listening; it rose and announced my presence.

Oh God. Oh my freaking God…what the hell am I doing?

I whirled, intending to sprint to my car, but the door opened.

"Kayla?"

Damn. I wished for invisibility as I turned to face him, though I would have settled for the earth fissuring under my feet. The image of him standing there wearing nothing but flannel pajama pants was enough to render me speechless. I'd never seen him in something so casual. I wondered if the fabric was as soft as I imagined. Soft flannel against hard man.

I shouldn't have come. I should have stayed far, far away.

"What are you doing here?"

"Honestly? I don't know."

He quirked a brow. "You don't know?" I shook my head, and the edge of his mouth turned up. "What do you want, Kayla?"

You.

Only I had no idea why. He was like a disease, and the bad cells had multiplied and taken over. He'd infiltrated my system, and now I couldn't get him out. Even now, standing in the freezing cold, my body flushed with warmth as I liquefied between my legs. Some crazy, destructive instinct rose within me, and I catapulted the last step and launched myself at him. Our mouths crashed together, open and hot and ravenous. We kissed like we were possessed, and maybe we were.

At least I was. I heard the door slam behind us an

instant before he released me.

"Get on your knees."

I fell to them without a second thought and reached for the waistband of all that soft flannel. Trembling with impatient desire—and maybe a little fear—I freed his cock and closed my mouth around him. A groan rumbled from his throat, evidence of his tightly held control. He grabbed my head, his hands shaking, and trapped me between them. No way would he allow me control—he was too close to losing it himself.

"Hands behind your back," he ground out between tight lips. I obeyed, and his eyes, so ridiculously blue, never left mine as he fucked my mouth. "Kayla…" His composure fell apart, and his hips took on the rhythm of madness.

I'd never felt so powerful.

He screwed his eyes shut and pushed to the back of my throat, roaring his release as his essence gushed into my mouth. Despite the fact that my panties were drenched, I gagged. Which only meant he shoved his cock deeper. His pleasure wouldn't be complete without my pain.

Still breathing irregularly, he pulled his pants up, and without a word, grabbed my hand. I followed him down to the basement. His fingers tightened around mine, as if he thought I might change my mind and bolt. I was considering it as we reached the last step. He'd had the damage repaired. The room looked as it always had; painful and cold. A dungeon indeed, though in this case I'd given away the key to my own freedom. I took one look at the St. Andrew's cross and remembered how he'd buried his face between my thighs, and all thoughts of cold evaporated.

He hoisted me against him, and we fell to the bed where he trapped me between his braced arms. "What's your safe word?"

I blinked. I hadn't expected him to give me one. "I-I don't know."

"You don't know much tonight, do you?"

"I know I want you."

His eyes widened, but then his face settled into the Gage I knew and loved to hate.

"I don't want to give you the option of telling me no, but I will. Last chance before I gag you and make you mine."

"I'm already yours." Anyone who could admit such a thing without breaking down must be insane. Which I was.

"Are you seriously arguing with me about a safe word?"

"Master—that's my safe word."

He laughed. "I might have to push you to your hard limits just to hear you say it."

"You could ask nicely."

He grabbed my left wrist and stretched it over my head. "I'm not nice."

"I'm not blind to how cruel you are, Gage." His name rolled off my tongue, forbidden. He clicked the locks in place and bent down to secure my ankles. I was still fully clothed.

"Don't gag me."

"I'll give you one request. Are you sure that's it?"

I scrambled to think of all the bad things. The whips, the nipple clamps, the butt plugs…actually, those weren't too horrible. I nodded. "I'm giving myself to you. Give me the right to cry or scream if I need to." I remembered Vegas and cringed.

Don't make me hold it all in again.

"Okay, no gags, but everything else is fair game."

With those words, he wielded a pocketknife and cut the clothes from my body. I'd been naked in front of him too many times to count, had lost all dignity in front of Ian and Katherine, but something about this time, this night, made me feel more vulnerable in my nudity. I was there of my own free will. He hadn't blackmailed or coaxed me; it was a truth I couldn't hide from, and being spread out before him brought it to the forefront of my mind.

He slid the flannel down his legs and stood tall, naked and unashamed. Gage was a lot of things, but ashamed wasn't one of them. His gaze traveled the length of my body, and his mouth turned up in a smile of conquer. He had me right where he wanted me, and suddenly I wondered if he'd been working toward this all along.

"If I asked you to let me go, would you?"

"If you say your safe word. You're not my slave anymore."

But I was, in all the ways that counted.

He crawled onto the bed and settled between my legs. "If you say it, I'll send you home."

I'd figured as much. It was all or nothing with him. "Sounds to me like establishing a safe word is pointless. If I don't do what you want, you'll just punish me for it by denying me." I yanked at my restraints, but he'd tightened them to the point where my limbs burned from the stretch.

He dropped his face to my stomach, his hair brushing my skin, lips and tongue teasing my belly button. "I don't want to deny you anything." His words vibrated against my belly. He lifted his head. "I want to make you come until you're screaming."

I had no doubt he'd succeed.

"But I like being in control." He dipped his fingers inside me. "If you can't live with that, then you need to leave now."

"I don't want to leave."

"Good, because I don't want you to either."

I couldn't think or breathe after that. He buried his head between my thighs and flicked his tongue across my clit, teasing for what seemed like forever until my fingers and toes were in a constant curl. He must have kept me in that state for an hour, lapping and swirling me to the edge while his fingers caressed my breasts. Unable to stand it any longer, I begged him with every moan.

He finally pulled away.

"Don't stop."

He ignored me and crossed to the other side of the basement, and when he approached the bed again, I knew the games were about to begin. He held three items in his hand; a butt plug, a nasty-looking set of nipple clamps, and a whip…*the* whip…the one he'd used the night he'd fucked me in front of Ian. It was long and thin, and I'd learned from experience how excruciating the strike of that thing was.

I started sobbing at the sight of it. "Don't."

He set the items on the bed, much too calmly, and watched as I pulled at my restraints. He didn't say anything, just waited until my body went limp and I gave up.

"Why?" I tasted the salt of my tears.

"Because I want you to trust me. I screwed up, Kayla." He picked up the whip. "Let me show you that you don't have to be scared of me. You have a safe word. Use it if you need to, and I'll stop."

"You don't need to do this."

"Yes, I do."

Something in the intensity of his expression terrified me, and I suddenly sensed that this was about more than earning my trust. This was the ultimate tipping point. Either I walked…or I stayed and gave him my pain. Pleasure for pain—it was the way he'd always operated, only now he was giving me a choice, and if I stayed, he really would own me.

He released my ankles and wrists. "Stand up."

I got up and stood before him, trembling and not knowing what to do or say.

Stupid! Say the word and go!

Pressing my lips together, I prepared to form the two syllables that would set me free, but the word lodged in my throat.

"Present your breasts."

"I-I'm not your slave anymore."

"I never said you were." The clamps dangled from his fist, big and clunky and painful-looking.

I folded my arms across my chest. "Why are you doing this?"

"This is who I am." His face hardened. "Hands behind your back now, or I'll make the whipping a punishment."

"There's a difference?"

"Yes, and you're going to learn what it is."

Go, go, go!

I couldn't budge, couldn't make my voice work. Slowly, I brought my hands behind me and clasped them together. He bent down and sucked at each nipple until they peaked. He took his time clamping them.

I gritted my teeth, squeezed my eyes shut and held my breath, but the pain didn't subside.

"Bend over the bed."

My mind shut down. It seemed like a bad dream, like someone else was obeying his every command. He slipped the plug in, and intense vibrations drowned out the agony of the clamps. And then he was whipping me, blazing caresses against my bottom. It hurt—I couldn't deny it—but he was holding back, and some of the strikes were so light, they were a tease.

"Stand up," he ordered.

I obeyed, but lost my balance and almost tipped over.

"Hold onto the footboard for support." He left a trail of fire down my right butt cheek, and I reached out and gripped the wood, breasts heavy and aching as the chain swung between them.

"Spread your legs."

His commands continued to come in clipped words, and I followed every one. I didn't allow myself to think beyond the sting of his whip. If I allowed awareness in, I knew I wouldn't like what I'd find. The strap snaked around my hip and kissed my crotch, eliciting a moan from my throat. He put more strength into it, and the caress became pain. I cried out—a plea for him to stop… a plea for him to continue.

"Master."

The whip thumped to the floor. "Is that your safe word?"

"I don't know." I shook my head. "No. Don't make me leave."

He pressed against me, chest to back, groin to buttocks, one hand pulling at the clamps as the other dipped inside wet need. "You're not going anywhere." His lips and tongue devoured my neck, and I moaned again, my center clenching as an orgasm built.

"I'm so close," I whispered.

"Not yet." He turned me around to face him. "Are you scared of me?"

"Yes." I said it without hesitation. I was scared of him all right—terrified of what he made me feel.

"You don't need to be." He grabbed the chain linking my breasts and tugged. "I want you in my bed." He picked me up and stomped up the steps, and as we entered his bedroom, I wondered how many other women he'd brought into this room. I couldn't stop from voicing the question.

He went rigid. "Why?"

"I'm curious." I sank into his mattress and stared up at him, waiting to see if he'd answer.

Our eyes connected and held. Long seconds passed, but he didn't answer until after he'd removed the clamps. "No one else has been in here but you." He plunged into me, and I was lost.

30. CONFESSIONS

Warm fingers feathered down my spine. I was sprawled on my stomach, sinking into the softness of the mattress and the allure of sleep. I hadn't slept late in a long time, but judging from the brightness behind my eyelids, I guessed it was at least nine. I snuggled closer to the warm body pressed against my side, glad that it was Saturday and I didn't have to get out of bed at the crack of dawn. He draped a leg over mine and splayed his fingers across my ass.

"Why did you cry last night?"

My eyes popped open, and I met Gage's questioning stare. "I don't know."

He swept my hair aside and kissed my shoulder. "Yes you do. I won't allow you to keep secrets from me. That hasn't changed."

I shrugged him off and scooted to the edge of the bed. "Last night was a mistake."

"You came to me, remember?"

I did remember, which made the light of day more

difficult to face. Every time I was near him, I lost another piece of myself. "I shouldn't have come."

"But you did, and you screamed while doing it."

"That's not what I meant, and you know it."

The bed dipped, and his fingers curled around my side. "Then why did you come back?"

"Because you live inside of me!" I jumped up and whirled around to face him. "I can't eat, I can't sleep, I can't get you out of my head. And this is so wrong. You're a fucking monster, Gage, and you keep pulling me in. Are you happy now?"

"I'm happy you're in my bed. I'm not happy that you're still fighting it."

"Fighting what?"

"You and me."

"There is no you and me!" I searched the floor for my clothes until I remembered that he'd cut them from my body. "I need something to wear. I have to be at the hospital soon." Eve was coming home today, and I didn't have the time or energy to argue with him. Her discharge changed everything. This had to end.

He slid out of bed and opened the door to a walk-in closet bigger than my bathroom. "Not the most fashionable, but they should fit." He handed me a pair of sweatpants with a drawstring waist and a large T-shirt. "You look sexy in anything you wear."

I clutched them to my bare chest and inhaled a whiff of the detergent he used. Damn him. That scent would always remind me of him. Avoiding his gaze, I dressed quickly and left his bedroom. Taking a detour to the basement, I wedged my feet into my shoes and headed toward the front door. He followed, completely naked, his towering form on my heels the whole way. I reached for the handle, but he pulled me against him.

"Stop fighting it, Kayla."

"It's just sex."

"Didn't we already have this conversation?"

I glared at him. "Apparently you need to hear it again. I'm not in love with you."

"I never said you were. This isn't about love. It's about connecting, and you damn well know we connect."

"Again…*just* sex." I pushed against him, but he refused to let go. "You're the last person I want around my daughter. She deserves better." *I* deserved better. "I'm done here." I untangled myself from his arms.

He smirked and leaned in until our noses almost touched. "You'll be back."

"I won't." I left the house, slid into the driver's seat of my car, and met his steady gaze from across the driveway. God, the man stood buck-naked in his doorway. He truly had no shame. A knowing glint lingered in the depths of his sapphire eyes. Smug bastard. He was one hundred percent certain I'd be back, begging him to take me.

At that precise moment, I knew he was right. I'd come back again and again, a glutton for his sadism. I'd lie down and let him do whatever he wanted—I was that addicted to him. I could think of no other way out, other than going cold turkey. I'd have to leave town—that seemed the best way to wash him from my life. Leaving wasn't going to be easy. I'd need to make preparations, get clearance from Eve's doctor, and find a place with an excellent children's cancer treatment center.

It was going to take some time and a lot of creative penny pinching, but I could do this...I only hoped he didn't ruin me in the meantime.

I backed down his driveway, and on my way to the hospital, I stopped by my apartment to shower and change. Eve was already picking at her lunch tray when I entered her room. Ian sat next to her, his bagged lunch open in his lap. They were watching Dora, and something about seeing a grown man watch a cartoon with a three-year-old floored me. This wasn't the first time I'd found him in her room, sharing lunch or playing a game with her.

Spotting me in the doorway, she broke into a huge smile. She jumped from bed and crashed into my arms with the power of a locomotive. The urge to cry overwhelmed me. Happy tears because Eve was healthy again, and desperate tears because I was so mixed up on the inside. I pushed it down and focused on her, on this day—the day she was coming home. She'd come so far. Just four weeks ago, I'd thought she wasn't going to make it.

I had Gage to thank for the reality of her in my arms.

"Hi, baby. Sorry I'm late." I deposited her in bed and took the seat next to her. "What're you having for lunch?"

"Yucky peas." She made a face, and I laughed.

Ian grinned at me from the other side of her bed. "No amount of bribing works. She won't touch them. She did eat the macaroni and cheese though." He rose to his feet and gestured toward the door. "Can I talk to you for a minute?"

"Sure." I swallowed my nervousness as he ushered me into the hall. He guided me down the corridor to where the elevators where. "Where are we going?" I asked.

"My office. We need some privacy for this conversation."

I already dreaded what was coming. He'd given me plenty of space during the past two weeks, never voicing the questions he tried to hide. Apparently, that was about to change. We descended two floors, and he led me down a maze of hallways.

"How do you keep from getting lost?"

His mouth turned up as he unlocked the door to what I guessed was his office. "Trust me, I still get lost sometimes." We entered a small, tidy space, and he pulled out a chair. "Have a seat."

I sat twiddling my thumbs as he settled next to me. "What's this about, Ian?" Something about the uncertain set of his mouth made my heart jump.

"I know the timing is shitty. You're about to bring Eve home, and this definitely isn't how I'd envisioned doing this…" He let out a breath and stood, and my heart started pounding when he bent to one knee. "But I love you, Kayla. I've spent the past seven years trying to right wrongs, trying to be good enough." He withdrew a white box from the pocket of his slacks and opened it to reveal a tasteful solitaire. "Marry me." His fingers curled around mine and squeezed. "I want to be here for you and Eve."

I blinked, but the room wouldn't stop spinning. His

face swam in my vision. "I…I can't."

"If this is about Gage…" He trailed off and lowered his head. "If it's about that last weekend you spent with him, I don't need to know about it. It's in the past. You did what you had to do. I understand that."

"You don't understand." My voice cracked, and when he looked up, my tears spilled over.

"You're in love with him? Kayla…what he did to you…

"I'm not in love with him." I blinked and prepared to spill my guts. I hadn't wanted him to know what I'd done, but he deserved the truth; at the very least, he deserved an explanation. "I went back to him last night. He didn't blackmail me, didn't force me. It was all me."

He glanced up, his pain evident in the firm set of his jaw. "I don't believe you."

I swiped rivulets of moisture from my cheeks. "I slept with him. I even let him whip me." Burying my face in my hands, I mumbled, "I don't deserve you."

He pulled my hands away. "Look at me."

"I'm going to leave town as soon as I can."

"No." He shook his head. "Don't leave. You mean everything to me. You think you don't deserve me? It's the other way around, Kayla." He swallowed, and his hands trembled as he dragged them through his hair. "I'm not innocent in all this. Whatever you feel for him…he brainwashed you, but I put you in that position."

I shook my head. "You didn't know he was blackmailing me. It was a simple hug. Gage went off the deep end all on his own and for no reason at all."

"I'm not talking about that. I'm talking about the reason he's doing this to you." He sucked in a deep breath. "I haven't been honest with you. There are things in my past I never told you about."

Suddenly, the subtle, white noise of the hospital roared in my ears; the soft scuff of sneakers padding down the hall, and the ticking of the clock above the door of his office. My gaze touched on everything but him—the framed degrees and certificates on the walls, the filing cabinets, and the picture sitting on the desk of an older woman with two little boys. Obviously, he shared the space with a colleague. Somewhere in the back of my mind, I realized how these inane thoughts provided a distraction. A much needed one, because no way was I ready to hear whatever he was about to say. He had yet to utter a word, yet I already felt the impact of what remained unspoken in the pit of my stomach.

He got up and paced the floor, growing more agitated with each step. "I was young and stupid, and I've lived with the shame for over a decade now. I've spent every moment since trying to make up for it."

I cleared my throat. "Make up for what?"

"I was sixteen, popular and on top of the world, and my parents idolized me. All my dad cared about was my future in football. I was barely a junior, but I already had scouts looking at me. One night…it was just one night, but that night changed everything. It's the reason I became a doctor."

"What are you trying to tell me?"

"I'm saying that everything he's done to you is my

fault." He fell into the chair beside me and dragged his hands through his hair. "I got drunk at a party...and was stupid enough to get behind the wheel."

A deep chill speared through me. "What happened?" I asked, my voice barely a whisper.

"I rolled the car." He buried his face in his hands for a moment, and when he looked up, his hazel eyes shone bright with the guilt he carried. "I had no business being with her in the first place, but she was older, and I fell hard."

I knew what was coming next. I knew, but I didn't want to hear it.

"Liz died. I killed her, and Gage has never forgiven me."

"How..." I cleared my throat. "How do you know him?"

He visibly gulped, as if he could swallow the words and keep them locked away forever. "He's my brother."

31. SURPRISE PARTY

Did everyone lie and keep secrets?

I unstrapped Eve from her car seat and helped her to her feet. She took off running toward our doorstep, and I scrambled to catch up with her, despising my state of distraction. "Eve, wait for mommy." I felt sick on the inside, disoriented, as if someone had turned me upside down and let all sense of reality tumble out. I couldn't form a coherent thought. It was all garbled words and phrases coming together in my head, and none of it made sense.

"Mommy, what's wrong?"

Even she could pick up on my chaotic state of mind. "Nothing, baby." I faked a smile for her sake and pushed the door open into our dark apartment. I flicked on the light, so distracted that I didn't realize anything was wrong until it was too late. The cold, hard barrel of a gun pressed into the back of my head, and though I couldn't see him, I immediately recognized the familiarity of his body pressing against my backside.

"Go to your room, Eve," he ordered. "I need to talk to mommy for a while."

Her wide eyes met mine, much too knowing for a three-year-old. A tear fell down my cheek as I forced another smile. "It's okay. Go. I bought you a doll. It's on your bed."

She hesitated, but the promise of a new toy lured her to safety.

Neither of us moved or said a word at first. The scent of his cologne, tarnished by the stench of whiskey, burned my nose. I swallowed the vomit rising in my throat. "What do you want?"

"What do you think I want?" he snapped.

"I don't know."

He snorted. "Don't play dumb. You know I can't stand it when you lie."

"I'm not lying. Please...don't hurt us." He nudged the barrel into my scalp, and I squeezed my eyes shut.

"I'd never hurt my daughter, but you're gonna pay." He pushed me further into the living room, but a knock on the front door halted him. "Fuck." Changing tactics, he tugged me in the direction of the door and folded his large body in the corner, keeping the gun trained on me. "Expecting someone?"

I shook my head.

"Good. Get rid of them." His gaze, colorless in a face that was too quick to deceive, leveled me. "Don't do anything stupid."

I turned the handle and peered out, and as I met Gage's stare, every part of me froze. I wanted to beg for his help, but Rick still had his gun pressed into my back.

"We're not done yet, Kayla," Gage leaned forward. "You're nuts if you think you can show up on my doorstep and pretend it didn't happen."

I raised my hand to ward him off. "I just got home with Eve. Can we talk about this another time?"

His eyes narrowed and then traveled the length of my body. "Are you okay?"

"Yeah, I'm fine."

His attention darted behind me, and he scanned the small space of my foyer.

"You need to leave." I slammed the door.

"Smooth move," Rick admonished. "You suck at acting normal." He pushed me into the living room and toward the couch. "You better hope he doesn't come back." Knocking me to my knees, he muttered, "Stubborn whore."

"Don't do this. Please."

"Shut up." He bent me over the cushion and jerked my hands behind my back.

"Please, Rick."

Blinding pain exploded at my temple. "I said shut up."

"Please," I begged again as he secured my wrists with rope.

He whacked me on the other side of the head and grabbed my hair, pulling tight. "Did you enjoy fucking him?"

"He forced me."

"But you liked it, didn't you? You keep going back."

I struggled to breathe, but my fear was too intense.

"Did your fucking vows mean nothing? You think you can forget about me so easily?"

"No," I choked. "I haven't forgotten you."

He laughed, a sound that struck more terror in me than any strike from Gage. "I'll make sure you don't forget me." He got up, and his shoes thudded across the carpet. He dragged a chair to Eve's door and wedged it underneath the handle. "You didn't think I'd miss my daughter's homecoming, did you?" The floor vibrated as he neared. "You and me are gonna celebrate all right. You owe me three years of fucking, Kayla."

He kneeled behind me and wrenched up my skirt, and I started sobbing, barely able to see through my tears. "Don't do this—"

"Did he fuck you in the ass? I hear he has a thing for that."

He shoved my face into the cushion, smothering my cries, and suddenly the memories flooded me. I'd almost forgotten how many times he'd choked me, how he'd smothered me with a pillow on a nightly basis. So many times I thought I was going to die, but then he'd allow me a gasp of air before continuing his suffocation methods.

"I bet he did do you up the ass." He pushed my legs together, tugged my panties down, and I heard the slide of a zipper.

I struggled, my lungs burning for life as the futility of my situation fisted my heart. He pulled my head up, allowed me a shallow breath, and then forced my face into the cushion again. I was going to die. The certainty of it gripped me, and I was no longer scared of being raped. Death was far worse. Death would take me away from Eve.

Eve.

Would he leave me like this? Lifeless for her to find?

Or would he disappear with her?

Head up…another gasp of air…then lightheaded darkness.

A loud, splintering crash tore through the apartment, and his hold on my head lifted. With a hoarse sob, I jerked my face up and sucked in air. Sucked it in until my lungs were full and near bursting. A grunt sounded, followed by a bang against the wall, and I rolled around to find Gage and my ex locked in a struggle. Eve screamed from her bedroom, tiny fists pounding on the door, and the chair shook under the force. I yanked at the rope binding my wrists, desperate to get to her, but the binding wouldn't budge.

"Stop it!" I yelled as the barrel inched toward Gage's head. They were engaged in a war, both exerting their strength to gain control of the gun. Gage was taller, but Rick had some bulk on him. He managed to kick free of Rick's hold for a moment, and Rick jumped to his feet and swung the gun in my direction. Time stopped as I stared past the barrel into his cold eyes. Nothing lurked in their depths; no regret, no anger. Just…nothing.

How had I missed this side of him all those years ago? The side of him that ignored his daughter's screams as he prepared to kill me once and for all?

"Please," I whispered, one last plea for mercy.

He cocked the gun.

Gage leaped into action, face distorted in the scariest mask of rage I'd ever seen. He charged Rick, a bull with red in his sights. They fell to the floor again, rolling, fists pounding, frantic fingers scrambling in a tug-of-war for the gun. The blast tore through the air just as the blaring sirens became noticeable.

Rick got to his feet and staggered back. He focused on the blood swallowing the front of his jacket, and for a moment he was entranced by it, the gun dangling from his fingers in distraction. And then he focused his attention on the broken door. The screeching sirens grew louder with every second.

He bolted, and I took in Gage's still form lying a few feet from me, watched the crimson spread across my carpet, and the sirens drowned out the hysterical cries of an innocent three-year-old.

And I welcomed blackness.

32. THE PRICE OF SIN

Snow trickled from the sky three days after Gage was shot. Not so much that driving in it was impossible, but enough to cause a stir of excitement. Normally, I would have been out in the wintery flakes like everyone else, throwing snowballs at Eve while we built a snowman. I watched the wintery weather through the window of the cheap motel we'd been hiding in. Eve was taking a late morning nap. Check out time was an hour away.

I couldn't bring myself to move. I was too busy torturing myself with what-ifs, too busy being a coward because I still didn't know if Gage had lived or died. Three days…and I didn't know if he'd died saving our lives. What kind of person did that make me? I'd left the emergency room three nights ago and hadn't looked back, and my phone had been powered off since. Ian was probably frantic by now trying to get ahold of me. But reality wouldn't step aside forever. I reached for my cell and switched it on, and I dialed Ian's number. He answered immediately.

"Where are you?"

"In a motel."

"I've been going out of my mind, Kayla. You freaking disappeared from the ER. Don't do that to me again."

"Is…" I swallowed and tried again. "Is he okay?"

"He's going to make it. They had to operate, but he's recovering." A train's horn blasted in the background, and I released a breath. "Where are you?" he asked.

I blinked a tear down my cheek. "Doesn't matter. I'm leaving today."

"Not without saying goodbye, you aren't."

I rattled off the name of the motel.

"Don't go anywhere. I'll be there in twenty."

By the time he pulled into the parking lot, Eve was already in her car seat munching on a graham cracker. I tossed our meager belongings into the trunk and slammed the lid.

"I can't talk you into staying, can I?"

"No. Eve's been having nightmares every night. I think a new environment would be good for her." I'd had nightmares too—paralyzing recollections of Rick trying to kill me. I leaned against the bumper. "Is he really okay?"

"That's what they tell me. He won't see me, but I hear he's been asking for you." He rubbed his chin. "I shouldn't have asked you to marry me. It was…selfish. I knew you were dealing with some stuff, but I was scared of losing you."

I dropped my gaze to the ground and kicked at the snow. "It was so long ago. Maybe what we feel for each other is an echo of what we could've been. Maybe we've been holding on when it's time to let go."

He tilted my chin up, and a snowflake danced on my nose. "I can't control how you feel, but I know what's in here," he said, placing his fist over his heart. "You've been here forever. It's always been you." He paused and gave a stubborn shake of his head. "I distracted myself with work, but I've never been able to get you out of my head."

His words squeezed the breath from me. "Don't do this to me now. I won't change my mind about leaving."

"I know, and that's why I'm not going to stop you. I know you need time. Maybe I do too." He stepped close and framed my face between his hands, and the warmth of his body penetrated mine. "I meant what I said, though. I love you, and no amount of time is going to change that." He wound his arms around me, and we held on to each other for a while, neither of us paying attention to the snow collecting in our hair. Another guest of the motel left his room and gave us a curious look as he headed to his car. Vehicles crept along the road, and one braked, going into a slide before stopping.

I wanted to hold on to him forever, frozen in this cold environment as the warmth of him surrounded me.

"Don't let him hurt you again."

"He can't hurt me if I'm not here."

"You don't know him very well."

"Turns out I didn't know you either." I backed out of his embrace. "Why didn't you tell me he was your brother? You watched"—I blinked the image from my mind's eye, but it refused to disappear—"you watched him with me. You screwed Katherine when all you had to do was be honest."

He kept his eyes downcast, and the guilt he wrestled with pricked at the part of me that still cared about him. Still loved him even. "I was stunned…when you came into that basement and got to your knees…" He shook his head, apparently at a loss for words. "And then I realized what was at stake…Jesus, Kayla. Your freedom, Eve's life. You begged me to go along with it, and I couldn't deny you."

"But you didn't tell me. You had every opportunity to, but you didn't."

"Chalk it up to cowardice. He'd ripped a hole in your life and it was my fault." He pinched the bridge of his nose and closed his eyes. "I shouldn't have come back to town."

"Gage is a grown man. Don't beat yourself up over his actions. None of us are innocent, me included. I stole from him."

"To save your daughter. My crime killed someone. Yours saved the person you love most in this world."

"Doesn't make it right."

"No, but you shouldn't have a problem sleeping at night. At least, I hope you don't."

I refrained from answering—maybe someday I'd be able to let it all go. "Would you mind taking Eve to get something to eat? I could use an hour alone."

"You're going to see him, aren't you?"

I nodded. "I need to."

"There's something you should know. They found Rick, and when they arrested him, he turned everything he had on Gage over to the authorities. They've begun an investigation, and Gage is probably going to serve some time in jail."

"What about Jody?"

"They arrested her this morning."

I shook my head. "Typical. Of course Rick threw her under the rug. How did you find out about this?"

"They questioned me. The Feds didn't understand that Gage and I haven't talked in years. I expect they'll want to talk to you too." He grabbed Eve from the car before unbuckling her seat and pulling it out. "I'll meet up with you soon."

"Thanks, Ian."

I didn't budge for a full five minutes after he left. Finally sinking into the driver's seat, I pulled onto the road and took the long way to the hospital. I dreaded this visit. I had so much to say, so much to confront him about, and no words in mind. He didn't notice me at first, as he was too busy arguing with the nurse about taking his vitals, a deep scowl on his face. I stood in the doorway and stared at the flakes coming down outside his window.

"Get the doctor. I don't need my fucking vitals taken for the hundredth time—I need out of here *now*." And that's when he saw me. He froze, which gave the nurse the opportunity to complete her task. Noting the readings in his chart, she then frowned at him on her way out, making it clear he was not her favorite patient.

"Made anyone quit yet?" I forced a smile and took a

step toward him, hoping to break the tense silence.

"I'm working on it." He leaned back against the pillows and winced.

"How are you doing?" I asked.

"Not too bad, all things considered." He frowned. "I wasn't sure if you were going to come."

"I wasn't sure either." I wandered around the room, finally stalling in front of the window, and became entranced by the falling snow. "I wanted to thank you for saving us, but Eve and I are leaving and we won't be back." I turned to face him. "I'll leave my resignation on your desk before I go."

"So that's it? You're just going to leave?"

I nodded. "I think the best thing for us is to move on from here."

He let out a bitter laugh. "You mean move on from me."

"You're part of it, yes. But I want her to have a happy life. She's been through so much."

"So have you."

"You're partly to blame for that."

He clenched his jaw. "I'm aware of that."

"Why didn't you tell me Ian was your brother?"

His eyes rounded, an unguarded second in which he couldn't hide his reaction, but then he smoothed his features. "*Half* brother. His dad's a bastard. Couldn't stand me." He studied me for a moment. "What else did he have the guts to tell you?"

"He told me about Liz."

"And now you're thinking I did this to you as a means

of getting back at him."

"Didn't you?"

"It started out that way, Kayla. I won't lie. I wanted to make him pay. I still do." His attention veered past me, and he grew lost in memories of the past. "His old man got him off with a slap to the wrist. I wanted to hurt him all right."

"Maybe you should let it go."

"So that's what you think I should do? Let him get away with murder?"

"Like I've let you get away with beating and raping me?" My words brought his gaze back to mine. "You made me pay for his sins, Gage. Now let it go."

"Who's going to pay for mine?"

"I hear you are."

"Guess he's given you an earful. So you heard about the investigation?"

I folded my arms and nodded. "What I don't understand is why you did it. You're not hurting for money."

"Not now, but that wasn't the case during the recession. I did it to save the company." He paused. "I repaid every cent. That's when I realized Jody had been skimming too."

"Do I have to worry about going to jail, Gage?"

"No. I covered your tracks. If it comes up, I'll take the blame."

My mouth hung open. "Why would you do that?"

"You've paid enough. Go be with your daughter, Kayla."

That was one order from Gage Channing I could obey without hesitation. I stalled, my hand on the door handle as the heat of his gaze seared my back. "Goodbye, Gage."

EPILOGUE

One year later

"He's staring at your butt again."

"Stop it!" I hissed at Stacey. "He is not."

"Oh yes, honey," she drawled, her Texas accent pronounced, "he is."

I cranked my head to find that Stacey was right. Nate was a regular customer, and he focused on my ass now as if it looked tastier than the Gigi's breakfast special sitting in front of him.

"How are the eggs, Nate?"

He blinked and then lowered his head. "Great as always, Kayla."

Stacey snickered. "He'll ask you out eventually, mark my words."

I hoped not—it would save me the trouble of rejecting him. I'd waitressed at Gigi's for eight months now, and luckily most guys who pursued me quickly got the message. Stacey and I had gotten close, but she didn't know about my past. No one did, and that was part of the allure of starting over in a town where no one knew me.

Yet something was missing…or rather *someone*.

My demons had relocated with me. Both Gage and Ian stalked the shadows in my bedroom at night, and I spent too much time lying awake. Eve's nightmares lessened over time, but mine hadn't. It didn't matter if the days were getting easier to get through—it was during those few dark hours when echoes of the past haunted me that I realized how weak I still was.

How broken.

Thankfully, I couldn't say the same for Eve. She was doing well, physically and emotionally, and she continued to provide the brightest part of my day. She'd started preschool four months ago, and I'd watched her blossom since. Ian's phone calls also brightened my days, though lately the tone of them had changed. I knew he missed me, and I felt the same way, though I questioned what it was about him that I missed exactly. It was a myriad of things—the sense of security I always felt in his presence, the way his kiss set my head spinning, the fact that I trusted him with my daughter…I could fill pages upon pages.

I missed Gage for other reasons…reasons that reinforced how lonely I really was.

Once my shift ended, I said goodbye to Stacey and promised to meet her on Saturday for a movie. She also had a child—a boy a year older than Eve. They said they were getting married someday. We laughed about their innocent childhood dreams, but deep inside, the idea bothered me. Kids often said such things, but the thought of Eve ever getting married, of subjecting herself to the cruelty of a man, terrified me. I'd grown so distrustful and paranoid that it put the term "jaded" to shame.

On my way home, I picked Eve up from daycare. The last thing I expected was to find an unfamiliar vehicle in my driveway. My world screeched to a halt at the sight of the man who unfolded from it. He leaned against his door and waited as I let Eve out of her booster seat. I hoisted her in my arms and carried her toward the door.

"Hello, Kayla."

"Hi…" My head spun with the reality of his presence. An entire year had passed since I'd walked away from my old life, and somewhere deep inside, I'd always known he'd come for me, but I hadn't allowed myself to dwell on that eventuality.

"Can I come in?"

"Sure." I pushed the door open. The duplex was small, but the place offered more room than our apartment had back in Oregon. "Just let me put on a cartoon for Eve." I got her settled in the living room with a snack, and then I ushered him into the kitchen. He leaned against the counter and silently watched as I turned on the oven and arranged chicken breasts in a baking dish. I kept myself busy with mindless tasks for several minutes, my heart tap dancing the whole time.

He was suddenly behind me, his hands on mine, pressing them to the counter and halting my movements. "Stop."

I went still. It'd been so long since a man had touched me. Months, though it seemed more like years.

He wrapped his arms around me and buried his face against my neck, inhaling as if he'd thirsted for the scent of me. "I've missed you." He tightened his hold. "So much."

I closed my eyes and focused on the weight of his arms across my chest, rising and falling with every breath. "Why are you here?"

"Isn't it obvious?"

Several moments passed, and I finally spoke the words I wanted to say. "I've missed you too." I ran a finger along his forearm. "But—"

"Don't shut me out, Kayla."

Shutting him out was impossible. Always had been.

"Can you get a sitter for tonight?" he asked.

I nodded without thinking. Stacey would look after her, but why would I need a sitter? I voiced the question.

"Because I'm going to show you how much I've missed you." He reached into my purse and dug for a few moments until he produced my cell. He held it out. "Get a sitter."

My fingers curled around the phone, hesitating. I could send him away. He'd go—I knew he would. And I would go about my life in peace. In peace and alone, always keeping everyone outside the bubble I'd built, unable to let anyone in.

And I would never feel this way again.

Taking a deep breath, I opened the phone and dialed.

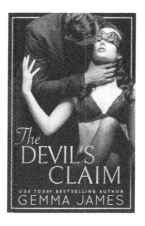

It's been a year since Kayla walked away from Gage Channing. Now he's back, and so is Ian Kaplan, Kayla's lover from her college days. Gage's jealousy is his worst enemy, and when he thinks Kayla has chosen Ian, he sets in motion a drastic plan to claim what's his. Only Kayla never expects him to infiltrate her heart so effortlessly, and she never dreamed there would come a day when he wouldn't want her.

Gage believes she's committed the ultimate sin, but will she use his mistake to finally escape the cage of his obsession? Or will she do whatever it takes to make him see he can entrust his heart to her…just as she's already lost the core of her being to him?

Please visit my website to find where you can purchase The Devil's Claim· www.authorgemmajames.com/books

Acknowledgments

For my husband, who doesn't enjoy reading but took the time to become invested in this story. Thanks for loving me, despite my craziness. To my kids, who understood that the headphones meant mom was at work. I have the best husband and kids in the world!

I also owe a huge thank-you to my best friend Crystal Richter. You've been there from the beginning tossing ideas back and forth with me. You're the most awesome friend anyone could ask for, and I love our late night trips to the coast. To my childhood friend Adria, who was the first person to read the beginning of what turned out to be a very bumpy ride! Thanks for believing in me, and I'm so glad I brought you over to the dark side!

And saving the best for last! Thanks to the readers, for without whom this story would have remained in the land of obscurity. Your words of encouragement and support mean more than you know. You guys continually amaze me with how much you've embraced this dark world my naughty muse created. Thanks for taking a chance on my work—you guys are the best!

About the Author

Gemma James is a USA Today bestselling author of a blend of genres, from new adult contemporary to dark romance. She loves to explore the darker side of human nature in her fiction, and she's morbidly curious about anything dark and edgy, from deviant sex to serial killers. Readers have described her stories as being "not for the faint of heart."

She warns you to heed their words! Her playground isn't full of rainbows and kittens, though she likes both. She lives in middle-of-nowhere Oregon with her husband, two children, and a gaggle of animals.

For more information on available titles, please visit www.authorgemmajames.com

Made in the USA
Las Vegas, NV
21 December 2023